TWELVE
SHOTS

TWELVE SHOTS

OUTSTANDING SHORT STORIES ABOUT GUNS

EDITED BY
HARRY MAZER

DELACORTE PRESS

Published by
Delacorte Press
Bantam Doubleday Dell Publishing Group, Inc.
1540 Broadway
New York, New York 10036

Library of Congress Cataloging-in-Publication Data
   Twelve shots : outstanding short stories about guns / edited by Harry Mazer.
         p.   cm.
         Contents: Briefcase / Walter Dean Myers—Cocked & locked / Chris
Lynch—Hunting bear / Kevin McColley—God's plan for Wolfie and X-Ray /
David Rice—Custody / Frederick Busch—Shotgun Cheatham's last night above
ground / Richard Peck—The war chest / Rob Thomas—Eat your enemy / Nancy
Springer—War game / Nancy Werlin—Until the day he died / Harry Mazer—
Fresh meat / Ron Koertge—Chalkman / Rita Williams-Garcia.
         ISBN 0-385-32238-0
         1. Children's stories, American.   [1. Firearms—Juvenile fiction.   2.
Firearms—Fiction.   3. Short stories.]   I. Mazer, Harry.
      PZ5.T86   1997
      [Fic]—dc21   96-37838
                                                                            CIP
                                                                            AC

The text of this book is set in 12-point Adobe Garamond.
Book design by Julie E. Baker

Manufactured in the United States of America
September 1997
10   9   8   7   6   5   4   3   2   1
BVG

*For George Nicholson, who was there at
the beginning, creating excitement when this book
was only an idea.*

*For Laura Hornik, whose comments and
suggestions were right on target and who guided
the book to completion.*

—H.M.

There was a little man, and he had a little gun,
And his bullets were made of lead, lead, lead:
He went to the brook, and saw a little duck,
And shot it through the head, head, head.

An old English nursery rhyme

CONTENTS

LETTER TO THE READER

Dear Reader,

I grew up in the city, and there were no guns in our house. But on the street, my friends and I were always playing gun games, pointing with a finger and "shooting." *Pow pow pow! Bam . . . Bang, you're dead.* We made guns, too: wooden pistols powered by rubber bands. They never shot straight, but they were guns. When you were hit you were "dead." In our games the "dead" always jumped up.

But something has changed in our country. Real guns are coming into the schools, and real kids are being shot by other real kids. Open the newspaper on any day, and read another story of someone shot. A student, stopping to ask for directions, is shot and killed by a frightened home owner. Cross fire kills a child going to the grocery store. A random bullet kills another child in his bedroom.

Handguns are cheap and available. Despite the occasional drives that encourage people to turn in their guns, more new guns enter the market each day. Technology and loose gun-control laws, added to a tradition of gun ownership, have made it possible for everyone who wants a gun to have one.

Kids have guns today in numbers they never had before. I'm talking about handguns. Not BB guns, not .22's, not hunting rifles, but Saturday Night Specials, guns that are easily purchased and easily concealed. Students show up in school with guns in their pockets and bookbags. Sometimes, accidentally or deliberately, the guns go off. Kids kill other kids. Kids kill themselves. The numbers are appalling. Turn to the back of this book to read the statistics.

The history of our nation is history with a gun. The gun allowed Europeans to seize this land. The gun lies deep in the American psyche. It is everywhere in the American story and it is everywhere in *Twelve Shots*. When I started this project, I asked a number of writers whose work I admired to write a story about teens and guns. Not the politics of the gun, not the heated arguments or the polemics, but the way guns are in fact present in people's lives.

When the stories started coming in, I read them with great excitement. Each was unique, fresh and quite wonderful. Every good story is about more than itself and these stories show it. I was surprised to find how many of them began with games. In our games we rehearse our lives, and in some of these stories we can see how guns work themselves into our psyches even as they work themselves into our hands.

David Rice's "God's Plan for Wolfie and X-Ray" is

the ultimate fantasy gun story, complete with Hallow-een costumes, real guns, and grown-ups to rob. Imag-ine a small town where two boys, known to everyone as a little *loco,* are inspired by a lifetime of TV shows to rob a convenience store. It's all playtime, until the guns start going off.

Nancy Werlin's complex story "War Game" is about the group and the individual, and the rules we must follow to survive. It starts with an elaborate water pistol war between two "armies" of kids. Jo, the master strategist, has a secret friendship, apart from the group. But all is put in jeopardy when her secret friend, Lije, is targeted by the group.

In the extraordinary "Chalkman" by Rita Williams-Garcia, there are no visible guns, not even toy guns, only children playing with a piece of chalk dropped by a police coroner. It's a city story in which children transform horror into a game.

After these street stories, it was almost reassuring to read Nancy Springer's "Eat Your Enemy," a fam-ily tale in which a father insists that his daughter learn how to handle a pistol. A stark story, it raises the question: In a world of violence, is the gun al-ways the enemy?

Frederick Busch's disturbing story "Custody" is also about a family, one split by divorce and acrimony. Taken away in the night by his father, whom he loves, Pete isn't sure where he belongs. Add a gun and you have a story about to explode.

Not all gun stories are grim. Richard Peck's "Shotgun Cheatham's Last Night Above Ground" is a tongue-in-cheek tall tale, at once a frontier story, a ghost story, and a gun story, in which a no-nonsense granny puts a smug city reporter in his place.

Like Richard Peck's story, Kevin McColley's "Hunting Bear" will make you laugh out loud. It's a spoof about guns and hunting and hunters, and about the urge to bring back the biggest trophy. Here, the bitten bites back. Or, as Gerry's grandfather says, "Every once in a while I like to read a story where the animal comes out on top."

Rob Thomas's "The War Chest" is a story about a wily old veteran, confined to a nursing home, who comes in contact with a young man there to do "good works." This is not your crusty-old-veteran-with-a-heart-of-gold story. The author, instead, asks you to think about the "glories" of war, comradeship, euthanasia, and the bitterness of old age.

My story, "Until the Day He Died," also deals with war, but in a very different way. As a boy, Mike dreams of glory. His games are war games. But it's no game when he parachutes out of his plane into enemy territory.

In Ron Koertge's "Fresh Meat," a boy gets his first rifle. There is ceremony here. We define ourselves by many things, but in this family, a boy's learning to shoot and handle a gun responsibly is the path to becoming a man. If you stand away from the story and think about the title, you may wonder about the story's deeper meaning.

Walter Dean Myers's "The Briefcase" takes place on crowded streets and packed subways. From the opening lines, the reader senses danger. A remark by a well-dressed stranger is taken as an insult by a bicycle messenger. This is a story not easily set aside, a story about lives in which rage builds, drop after drop, day after day.

Chris Lynch's "Cocked & Locked" is a frightening tale of friendship, love, and a deeply disturbed boy who "wears his insides on his outsides," a boy who is wild and unpredictable and who has a gun.

The gun is a fact. It has a weight and a smell and even a taste. Guns are devices made to do one thing, and they do it very well. Guns fire metal pellets that travel at high velocities with enormous energy, but without passion or discrimination, until the energy is dissipated or the pellets come in contact with an object. This is the reality of the gun.

Bullets are cheap. What's not cheap is life. A life, unlike a bullet, unlike a gun, is not easily produced. A bullet can end a life as easily as flipping a light switch, but a light switch can be reversed. No one has yet devised a way to make a bullet turn back.

Guns are not likely to disappear. They are here in our lives. How can we live with them? *Can* we live with them? Can we live without them? What's clear is that as their numbers increase, so does the danger for all of us. If no one had a gun, what would the world be like? We don't know. What we do know is that if everyone has a gun, no one is safe.

Harry Mazer
September 1997

BRIEFCASE

by Walter Dean Myers

Yo, man, like there's a way to deal with people. You know what I mean? You coming home from work and everything and you tired you don't need nobody just dissing you for nothing, right? You a bike messenger don't mean you ain't people. There was nothing on the delivery board so I locked my bike, got my radio, and told Manny that I would see him tomorrow like I always do.

I was like beat. Just before quitting time I had picked up a flat case from Broadway near Canal Street and had to take it all the way uptown to Riverside Drive. You go up Riverside Drive and that's like all uphill. Then I got caught up in traffic on the way downtown and some woman stepped right out in front of my bike. I stop and almost bust myself up and she call me a "menace." Now what's that supposed to mean? Like Dennis the Menace is like a kid and I ain't no kid. What come through my mind is to get off the bike and slap her face for her but she wasn't even worth it. You know what I mean?

So when I left the joint I head over to the A train going out to Brooklyn. I'm still thinking about that woman and I'm thinking maybe she's a foreigner or something and maybe that was a foreign word or something. Maybe "menace" was Spanish or Russian or something and meant something else. If I see her again I'm going to stop her and ask her what she meant by that.

So the A train come and I get on and it's like really crowded but I don't stink or nothing because I use deodorant and anyway I don't sweat a lot. It's a long ride out to Rockaway Avenue so I put my radio on and I'm minding my business when this guy taps me on the shoulder.

"Can't you turn that radio down some?" he says.

This guy is tall and brown skinned and carrying a briefcase like he think he somebody. I look around and everybody is looking at me.

I turned the radio off. You know, I got some nice jams but he got me out of the mood even to listen to them. Man, I give this sucker a look like daggers coming dead at him. Who he think he is? He's clean but he ain't all that, you hear what I'm saying? And he definitely ain't all he think he is.

He wearing glasses and he keep turning and peeking out from behind his four-eyed self at me. My eyes were dead on him. Half the people around us was white and that's why I think he dissed me. You know, some brothers like to diss black people in front of whites. That's how they get they thing off.

He got off at Hoyt and Schermerhorn and I looked at him walking toward the stairs. Fool couldn't even walk right. I turn my radio back on and sat down. The jams didn't even sound right because that fool got me all messed around.

The block was jumping. Little Jimmy, the guy who work in the barbershop, was standing on the corner and I asked him what was happening.

"Two guys beat up Pookie," he said.

"Little Pookie?" I asked. "Why they do that?"

"They said he took some money from their cousin," he said.

Pookie was cool. I didn't know him that good because I stay to myself but from what I see he gives everybody they propers. Maybe he took they cousin's money and maybe he didn't. But they shouldn't be beating on him. Somebody beat on you they saying you a punk. You can't walk around being no punk.

What I was thinking was that I hang on the corner for a while then I'd cop some fried chicken for me and my moms, go home, and watch some television. So I was hanging, checking out the happenings and listening to my jams when I see some people standing around talking to these two dudes. One of them is a big cornbread sucker they call Billy and the other one was Darnell.

"They the guys that beat up Pookie," Little Jimmy said.

There was a argument in the corner store where the Koreans sold newspapers and stuff. Soon as the Koreans get into a argument they call the cops. Square business. Then you see the cops come and the Koreans get all excited and everybody goofs on them and then the cops leave and stuff gets back to regular until the next argument starts. I'm checking out the Koreans arguing with some sister about how come she can't found out what the lottery number was last month's and I'm steady goofing on the whole scene. Then the cops show like they always do and they go inside the store. Then, from down the street toward the Avenue, I hear some more goings-on.

"Yo, punk! How you like me now!"

I turn and I see Pookie and he got a swoll-up eye and his shirt is torn and dirty. But he got a gun, it look like a chrome and he standing there pointing it at the dudes who had beat him up.

Man, guys was diving every which way. Trying to get out the way.

Blip! Blip!

Pookie blasted off two caps. People were screaming and stuff and then the two cops which was in the Korean store come out and Pookie run down the street and they was running after him. I went out into the street to see what was happening and I saw the cops running after Pookie with they guns out but Pookie was getting up, you know what I mean? The brother was doing some heavy footing. He had his head back and his arms was pumping strong. I look back to where the scene went down and I seen a kid stretched out. The cops was running and holding down their holsters so they wouldn't flop and stuff. I watched until first Pookie and then the cops went around the corner.

"They ain't gonna catch that dude," a brown-skinned kid said.

"Word!" I gave the kid five and moved on. You got to keep moving on.

I got the chicken and went home but my moms wasn't there. I forgot it was Monday and her church night so I scoffed down the chicken and watched me some television. Then I went down to the corner to see what was happening and that's when I heard that they got Pookie.

"They caught him hiding behind a Dumpster on Macon Street," a fat girl said. She was dressed nice with some silver pants and a black blouse that was smoking. "But they didn't find the gun," she went on. "They looked all over and even in the Dumpster but they still didn't find it so I think they ain't got nothing on him."

"He hit that little girl." Little Jimmy was still hanging out. "She ain't hurt bad but if it makes the newspaper then they going to put Pookie in jail. If it don't make the paper he okay."

"She ain't hurt bad," the fat girl said. "The bullet just hit her arm. She was just scared."

She was looking at me and smiling and everything but I don't go out with no fat women. That's just the way I am. A chick want to go out with me she got to be fine.

Next day was slow. Manny said things was getting real slow because of the fax machines. Mostly we carrying big packages that you got to balance on the bike. You can't make any money carrying big stuff like that because you can't carry enough in your pack. Then you run into dudes who want you to go round the delivery entrance and waste your time.

After work I walk with my man Omar down to the subway. He live uptown and so he got the first train and I got the downtown A train again. Who I see? That same dude who dissed me the day before. He had that same briefcase with him. Bet he didn't have nothing in that briefcase but some old newspapers or something. He looked dead at me and he recognized me. I had my radio but I didn't have it on. Then he turn his back to me and started talking to some people he was with. Two was white and one was black. You could see they all thought they was above everybody. He was wearing a charcoal-gray suit and a pink shirt. That showed he didn't think nothing of his manhood. You don't bust out with no pink shirt *and* carrying some briefcase.

When we got down to the World Trade Center his friends got off and only Mr. Briefcase was left. I knew he was going to look over at me and he did. He thought I was going to look away, like he was so much

I didn't even dare look at his face, but I fooled him. I stared right back at him. I was sitting down but when he got off at Schermerhorn I got up and walked to the door and looked out at him so he would know that I wasn't scared of him or nothing.

He was big. You know, he looked like one of them college boys. Some of them maybe played some ball or something.

That don't worry me. I can use my hands. I ain't no Mike Tyson but I don't punk down. You hear what I'm saying?

He was probably going home and thinking about me and how he had a good job and I was just a messenger. Sometimes you deliver a message or a package and you find people like that. Sometimes they don't even say nothing to you, just point to where you supposed to put down the package. Then when you go they say to they secretary how they just pointed to the desk and you had to put the package down and leave and then they crack on that like you a big joke or something.

I just wiped that dude right out my mind. I meditated him out my mind like he didn't even exist. Fool was never even born.

Nothing was shaking on the block. Little Jimmy wasn't around and I saw the fat woman who was talking the day before and I said hello to her and she said hello to me and she had a nice smile which she flashed on me but I didn't let it go to my head or nothing.

"So you hear anything about Pookie?" I asked.

"His sister said they got him locked up and charging him with a shooting down at the projects," she said.

"Down at the projects?"

"Yeah," she said. " 'Cause they didn't find the gun he had the other day and the brothers he shot at didn't press no charges."

"The projects near St. John's?"

"Uh-huh."

"I don't even think Pookie hang out down there," I said.

"You know how the cops are," she said.

Yeah, I knew that, but I didn't know how they caught Pookie because he was really getting up when I saw him. He must have caught a cramp or something.

There wasn't much on television so I took a walk. I went on down to Macon Street and looked around. There were two Dumpsters down there and I tried to figure out how they could have caught Pookie. One Dumpster was filled with garbage and the other one was filled with old furniture. I thought about looking around to see if I saw the gun but then I remembered the woman said the cops looked in it.

When I got back to the block it was raining. The barbecue joint was just opening and the guy who run it looked at me waiting to cross the street. He was probably thinking that I looked stupid standing in the rain because I didn't have a umbrella. He didn't know what I had. People just jump up and start thinking things about you and they don't know a thing. That just makes you mad and then they walk away.

I went upstairs and looked around until I found my umbrella. I got two umbrellas. One is a push-button number which I take around when I'm just out styling or with a chick. The other one is a small one I keep in my bag when I'm making deliveries. I took out the push-button one and went back downstairs and went in front of the barbecue joint and opened it. Let him see that I had a better umbrella then he did. He thought I was thinking that he was rich just because he had a barbecue joint but he didn't impress me. He might have been bankrupt or a freak. A lot of freaks have restaurants.

"Where you been?" my moms asked when I got home.

"Out," I said. "Just walking around."

"You eat anything?"

"Uh-huh."

I watched some television while she did some knitting which is what she like to do. They had on a show about cops and I got to thinking about Pookie again. If they didn't find the gun he must have thrown it somewhere. Maybe the cops didn't look hard enough in the Dumpster. I thought maybe when I got off work tomorrow I could go and look in the Dumpster and see if they missed it.

*   *   *

Betty is a girl that works in the office. Usually she sit behind the rail at a desk next to the one Manny use sometime. But when I got in she was outside of the rail where the benches be. We call that the pit and that's where the bikers hang out waiting for jobs. Mostly the office people don't come out there. They just hand the packages to us over the rail. Betty was talking about she didn't know what happened to the bikes.

"What happened?" I asked.

"Two bikes got flat tires."

"My tires were flat and Omar's tires were flat," Gene said.

My tires wasn't flat when I checked them. Omar's tires and Gene's tires wasn't cut, just flat. Somebody was messing around and I didn't know who it was but I knew it wasn't me. Then Manny come out and started putting slips on the board. You had to pick up the slips and then sign out the deliveries on a form from Betty. But once you had the messages signed out you had to be on your way within two minutes or give them up.

Omar and Gene was trying to pump up they tires with a little hand pump and rolling their eyes at me like I done something. I felt sorry for them but I had to get paid so I got the slips from the "Two" zone which was between Sixtieth Street and Seventy-fifth on the West Side. Everybody wanted the "Two" zone because you didn't have all the tall buildings and security to deal with. Most of the places in the "Two" zone were stores or studios. You just bust in, deliver the message or package, have the people sign for them, and you split. I didn't have no hassle all day except for a meat truck that cut me off.

When I knocked off it was a quarter to five even though I hadn't made a real trip since about three o'clock. I delivered one flat to a clothing store next to Radio City. I had some nice money in my pocket. I thought about stopping and getting soda and maybe talking to the fat woman and checking her out to see if she was for real or not. There was a dude begging in the subway and he came on to me with "Yo, brother," but I wasn't going for it. Those dudes who be begging could have a bank account and stocks and bonds and anything, then when you give them a quarter they wait until you leave then they laugh at you. They got all that money and you giving up yours.

I look for Briefcase in the subway. He wasn't on the platform. The time was just five o'clock, that was when he usually showed up. I walked up and down the platform but he wasn't there and I let a train go by. Then the two white dudes he was with that time came and he wasn't with them. I let that train go by and got on the next one and the chump still didn't show.

He probably took a taxicab. That's what some dudes who want to play big time do. They hop in a cab and when the cab driver ask them where they want to go they give them a faraway place like they don't

care about how much money it cost. I had enough
money in my pocket to go to Brooklyn in a cab but I
wasn't trying to play no big time.

Or maybe he sitting in a bar some place and talking
about how people ride the trains playing they radios
and stuff. "Some people don't know how to act and
they got they radios on too loud." That's just the kind
of thing a punk like him would say.

Nothing was shaking in the hood. I saw the fat
woman again and asked her name. She said it was
Cheryl, which is a pretty name. But then she smiled at
me like I was supposed to be all impressed or thinking
I'm in love or something. No way.

I laid some money on my moms and she said thank
you and then I watched some television except when
she fixed something to eat and I got down with that.
Moms could definitely burn some soul food.

In the middle of the night I woke up. I remember
Cheryl saying that they found Pookie hiding near the
Dumpster and the cops looked in the Dumpster. She
didn't say nothing about them looking *under* that bad
boy.

I got up and dressed. Moms was sleeping and I
could hear her breathing. She was almost snoring but
it wasn't exactly a snore so much as it was hard breathing. I locked the door and went on downstairs and it
was hot out. The air wasn't even moving and some
people were still on the stoop.

The Dumpsters were three blocks down and one
block over and I went over and looked at them. The

one with garbage in it was down on the ground and you couldn't get nothing under it if you wanted to. The other one was off the ground a little and I got down and looked under it. I couldn't see nothing. I didn't want to put my hand under there so I looked around and then I found a stick. I put the stick under the Dumpster and pulled it around. All that came out was some old food wrappers, a milk container, and a piece of a brick.

"What you doing?" An old dude was standing over me. "You lose something?"

"I dropped a quarter," I said.

"You ain't going to get it with that stick," he said.

"I got to try," I said.

"I guess you do," he said. "You be better off coming round in the morning."

Then he went on.

I dragged the stick a couple of times more and nothing came out. Then I was going to leave when I looked at the first stuff I pulled out. There was nothing in the food wrappers but the milk carton was heavy. It was smashed down some but when I looked at the top it was split open and there was something in it. I dumped it out into my hand.

All the way home I wanted to run and get into the house to see if it was real. What I did was to walk cool, though, because I didn't want to draw attention to myself. When I got inside I went into the bathroom, put the milk container on the hamper, and washed my hands.

"That you in there?" my moms called out.

"Yeah," I said. "I went out for a walk."

"Oh, okay," she said.

Then I listened while she went on back in the bed-room.

I took the gun out of the milk container. On the side it read Taurus PT-58. It felt good in my hand. It was steel with wood on the side. I held it in my hand and looked in the mirror. I turned out the light and opened the bathroom door just a little. Then I looked in the mirror again and I could hardly see myself. I could see my eyes and one side of my face and even though I couldn't see the gun I could tell I was hold-ing it.

I wrapped the gun in a lot of toilet tissue and put it in my pocket and put the milk container in the gar-bage before I went to my room. The gun was hard under my pillow but I wanted to make sure I knew where it was.

Sometimes people see you and they don't like you. First they say some little thing to you, like "What you looking at?" or "Why you making so much noise?" Something like that. Then if they think they can chump you off they come up to you and get up in your face. Nothing you can do except get ready be-cause they got they minds made up to chump you off, maybe punch you in the face or something like that.

I didn't get "Two" zone. What I got was "Five"

zone which was mostly around Forty-second Street.
That used to be a good zone when all the hookers
worked there because they give you tips. It was still
okay, and I made a lot of deliveries. One delivery I
made was to Pier 80. It was mostly deserted except for
the office but there was a bathroom and I went in
there and peed. Then I looked outside and nobody
was around and then I went back in the bathroom and
took the gun out. I pointed the gun into the garbage
can and went to pull the trigger. It didn't move. I took
it out and looked at it. I looked for the safety. There
was a little lever on the side. I moved it and pointed
the gun back into the garbage and pulled the trigger
again. It was harder than I thought. When it went off
it didn't make as much noise as I thought it would,
but it got me nervous. It didn't get me scared because
things don't scare me. I just left the bathroom with the
gun in my pack and started out to where my bicycle
was locked up.

I couldn't help thinking about Briefcase. I knew he
was thinking about me, wondering what was going on
in my mind, wondering if he could just chump me off.
Maybe he just tried to put me out his mind like I was
nothing. That's the way he thought about me, like I
was nothing. I was nothing because he could just walk
away from me and didn't have to think about who I
was. He got his briefcase and his house with nine locks
on the door and I couldn't get in to none of them.

Maybe he even thought he start a fight with me. If
he punched me out right there in the train station

everybody would go home and talk about it. How some dude all dressed up and carrying a briefcase had punched out a messenger. That's the way they would talk about it. A cool dude in a suit and carrying his important papers messed up a nothing sucker. Then he could go home and tell his wife, if a punk like him had a wife, how he had beat me up. Then she would get all steamy and happy like the women do on television.

I had seen Cheryl again. I was holding the gun in my pocket like I always did but I didn't say nothing to her.

"Pookie's stepfather said they charging him with all kinds of stuff," she said. "The police saying he was places doing things and he don't even know where the places is."

"That's cause they think he ain't nothing," I said. "He ain't nothing so they can mess over him."

She said, "Yeah, I know what you mean," and then went on down the street. It was wrong what they was doing to Pookie. They knew it, too.

All day at work I didn't have nothing to say to nobody, just did my runs and kept my mind on taking care of business. It was a long day and I got a upset stomach just before quitting time.

When I got to the subway I was nervous and my stomach was aching. I didn't see him when I got there, and I thought he might be trying to sneak up on me. But the thing the fool didn't know was that I was ready for him. I had my pack slung over my shoulder and one hand was inside the pack. If Briefcase wanted to mess with me I was ready.

The first A train came into the station and Briefcase still wasn't there. I looked at the time and it was time for him to get off work.

I thought maybe he had a knife or something. One of them fancy knives with all the attachments and stuff. Maybe he was waiting for the platform to get crowded and then he would come up and stick me. I was getting real nervous. It was even hard to breathe.

The next train came and at first I didn't see him. Then, just before the doors closed I saw him and I squeezed on. He was on the other side of the car with his face stuck up in a newspaper like he was so important. I could see him, but he didn't see me.

WALTER DEAN MYERS is the author of numerous award-winning fiction and nonfiction books for children and young adults, including *Hoops, Motown and Didi, The Outside Shot, Slam!,* and the Newbery Honor books *Somewhere in the Darkness* and *Scorpions.* He is a multiple winner and honor recipient of the Coretta Scott King Award, and in 1994 he won the Margaret A. Edwards Award for Outstanding Literature for Young Adults. Myers grew up in Harlem and now lives with his family in Jersey City, New Jersey.

"The major differences between the Harlem of my youth and the Harlem of today are the lack of jobs and the availability of guns," he says. "The great American tragedy, from my point of view, is black-on-black violence. Guns make that violence easy. People who commit crimes usually have to envision themselves in the performance prior to the actual event. No one goes from perfect innocence to armed robbery. The physical act that has to be performed—walking into the convenience store, getting up the nerve to say 'This is a stickup,' jumping over a bank counter—becomes a barrier to the act.

"When it comes to homicide, the barrier is lowered by the ease of the method. Clearly, the gun is the easiest method available. And guns are available in a quantity that is truly frightening."

COCKED & LOCKED

by Chris Lynch

"Tell me, Oakley," Pauly says.

"I will, Pauly," I say right back. "I'll tell you just as soon as you ask. But that's the way questions work, you have to ask me something first. Then I can tell you."

He'll do that if you don't stay on him. He'll float you a question without ever asking it, till you want to choke it out of him. He says he's a poet. Which, he says, explains everything.

I don't think it does. Nothing explains everything.

In fact, nothing explains Pauly. Except that he's my friend. Ever have a friend that nobody could figure out why you bother? Pauly's that friend for me. I'm the kid in Whitechurch that everybody says, "Good kid, that Oakley. Fine, quiet, polite boy. No trouble." People like that about a kid—no trouble—more than they like anything else. Pauly's the other kind. "There goes a mistake waitin' to happen" about sums up people's opinion of Paul.

The difference? I don't show my insides to anybody. Don't, can't, won't. If you're like that, people seem to appreciate you for it. Pauly boy on the other hand wears his insides on his outsides, and nobody nowhere is ever comfortable with that.

Somewhere in there we're a match, Pauly and me.

We are perched on the slope of a small green hill.

We are always perched on the slope of a small green hill. Whitechurch is completely surrounded, hemmed, by small green hills. Locals compare it to Rome. I've never seen Rome, but I suspect that this is a stretch. From where I sit, the town seems more like a bathtub. Ever seen a mouse get caught in a bathtub? He clicks and scratches and flails his little nailed feet a million miles an hour trying to get up the enamel walls of the tub, but he keeps sliding back down. Then he either quits and just cools out in the bottom, or he never gets it, and he runs until he has a heart attack. Sitting on the hills is like sitting on the edge of the tub, watching the mouse.

We're overlooking my buddy Pauly's most favorite of all favorite places in Whitechurch. The prison. There's some milling about going on in the yard, but since this is Thursday afternoon, it's not the prisoners doing the milling, but guards and police and prison officials practicing their fife-and-drum stuff.

They're god-awful. We never miss it.

"Okay," Pauly says. "Just a what-if. What if, if a

guy wanted to pick one off. You think somebody could do that, and get away with it?"

"A cop? Pauly, you asking me if you could shoot a cop and nobody would mind?"

"Of course not," he says, sticking a sharp elbow into my side. "You think I'm a dope?"

A lot of times I do, I do think he's a dope. But I don't ever say it to him because I figure he's heard it enough times from almost everybody else in town.

"No," Pauly continues. "I mean, a con. What if somebody got the idea to drop a prisoner, right down there in the yard? Would anybody really mind, do you think?"

I turn toward Pauly to see if he's joking, but there isn't a joke anywhere in him. He keeps staring down at the yard.

"Ya, Pauly. I think somebody'd mind. Probably, somebody'd mind a lot."

Pauly waits a long time, staring off, listening to the fife and drum—and bagpipe, actually—strangle some innocent song to death.

"I don't see why," Pauly says. "I really don't think people would care much."

In the yard below us, the leader of the police group is screaming and throwing his baton against the twenty-foot-high fence. Like he does every week.

"Of *course* you're bored," he yells at the pipers. "We only know the one goddamn song. Who the hell wants to play 'Loch Lomond' fifteen hundred times? Ya bunch a dopes."

Pauly's eyes narrow. "What about him?" he asks, pointing at the yeller.

"They might not care much," I sigh, "but they'd still notice."

"See, that's what I think about the criminals. I think maybe people would notice if you did one of them, you'd get noticed for it, but in the end, nobody'd get pissed off about it. Which would be kind of slick in the end, don't you think?"

Lilly #7

she's LEAving me red
VIolence is blue
WHITEchurch is brown
there's a fuckin ROCK in my shoe

—by paulY

"Don't you ever get angry, Oakley?"

This is Lilly, who is smiling and who is Pauly's girlfriend, even though she spends way more time with me than she does with him. She's big and bulky and dark and quite special if you pay close enough attention. She's awfully plain if you don't. We're together this March afternoon, hanging out and finding out, up on the faraway hill next to the cider press building that wouldn't be pressing anything until the next leaf-peeping busload came by in the fall. This particular press is located on this particular hill because this is the best looking-spot for people to overspy our little kingdom while they sip their fresh juices. The view down Press Hill is what Whitechurch wants to look like. Cider is what we want to taste like.

Pauly hates apples so much, you'd think they were a disease.

"Of course I get angry," I answer Lilly. "What kind of a question is that?"

"It's a regular question, is all. Because if you do get angry, it's angry in a way I can't see."

And Lilly likes to be able to see all. Lilly likes things in plain sight where she can see them.

"You mean, like Pauly gets angry?" I ask her. The question I'm not supposed to ask. That's why I'm special to her, because I don't usually ask.

"Don't, Oakley," she says, and starts down the hill. I start after her.

"Fine, then, I won't," I say. "Come on back up the hill with me. I'll behave and be quiet."

She comes back up the hill and sits beside me again. "I have to go in a few minutes anyway," she tells me. "Baby-sitting for the Rev."

I nod, which is my best thing. I sit, and I behave. Because there is nothing I like better than sitting on the hill doing nothing on a nice day while Lilly sits close beside me doing nothing too. Some guys—like Pauly, and like a lot of the older guys at the high school—don't seem to appreciate this, doing nothing. But that's not me. I'm doing all the nothing I can while I can because I can feel it coming, the day when I have to do *something*.

But then, for no reason, I make the trouble again.

"So, what does he do, Lilly?" I ask. "You want to tell me what he does when he's angry?"

And that's that. Without speaking, she gets up, brushes old yellow grass off her seat, and heads down the hill, straight down toward the white church of Whitechurch, where the Reverend and his wife and their baby live in the shadow of the valley.

I know I've done it, exploded the good thing we have up on Press Hill, and I don't even try to make good. I just follow along behind Lilly as she breaks into a jog down the decline, and before we reach the Texaco at the foot, she will have let me catch up.

"Yo" comes the holler from back up where we'd just left.

Pauly, of course.

"Stop right there, you two," he yells, pointing down on us like Moses or somebody.

There is nothing between me and Lilly, and Pauly knows it. Nothing but being friends, anyway. It was just that if Pauly was your best friend like he is with me, or if he was your boyfriend like he is with her, then you'd find yourself needing somebody else to talk to on a regular basis.

I'm that for Lilly, and she's that for me. Pauly doesn't care at all, the way a lot of guys would if their best friends seemed to be bird-dogging their girls. In fact, he seems to enjoy the setup.

"You, and you, come over here to me right this

minute," Pauly says, pointing at the piece of Press Hill right in front of him.

I'm staring at him, thinking of walking back up there, when Lilly grabs my hand and yanks me along, laughing like a mad thing. We speed, like a couple of boulders hurtling down the steep grade, until I'm sure I'm going to lose it and wind up with a mouth full of turf.

Pauly tries a little, screaming and chasing a short ways, but he doesn't have a chance. Always caught a couple of steps behind, our Pauly.

At the Reverend's house, Lilly and I are sitting on the sofa across from the window seat in the curved alcove that looks out over the yard. The baby is sleeping. The baby is always sleeping. We are watching a movie on cable, but not really watching it. I do this thing—and I think Lilly does it too, but to ask would be to shatter it—where I watch the famous stars on the TV screen, but I don't listen to a thing they say, and I don't think at all about what's happening to them in the plot. For sound track, I listen to Lilly, and to myself, and we and the stars mesh all up together.

"If your life was a movie, who would star in it?" Lilly asks me as she passes the tortilla chips.

I've only thought about this a hundred thousand times, but that doesn't make the answer come any quicker. The players keep changing, most of them.

"Sylvester Stallone would play my mother," I say as I pass her my Coke.

Lilly slaps me on the arm and says, "That's not funny," while she laughs.

"I wasn't joking," I say.

"All right, Stallone plays your mother. Who plays you, then?"

I nod confidently. "Sylvester Stallone," I say. "Disney'll do it."

Lilly snatches the chips back from me. "Pretty bent, when you think about it, Oakley," she says. "Maybe we should talk about this a little more."

"Maybe not," I say. "So who's in *your* movie?"

"Audrey Hepburn," Lilly says. "But when she was alive, of course. Like in *Wait Until Dark,* where she was blind."

Lilly isn't blind. Unless she really believes she looks like Audrey Hepburn. She's more like two Audrey Hepburns, but that isn't important at all. The stuff that makes her someone you want to get next to is mostly invisible, Lilly stuff.

Lilly #31

If Violence is blue
and my lilly is pink
which Motion would move her
which Potion should I drink?

—by paulY

"What about him?" I ask, pointing across the room, over the window seat, through the window and out into the backyard where our Pauly dances up and down for our amusement. Pauly's forbidden to enter the Reverend's house. He's got a good soul in there somewhere, the Rev says, but he's never going to cross *this* threshold. Whatever that means.

"So who plays him?" I ask again.

Pauly rushes up to the window, climbs up on the woodpile and presses his face to the glass.

"Pauly's not going to be in my movie," Lilly says seriously.

I wave to him. "Hey, Pauly," I say.

"Go ahead," he calls, muffled, through the glass. "Go on and kiss her if you want to."

"I never said I wanted to," I reply, all indignant. I'm not fooling anyone, though.

"Hey," Lilly snaps. "What do you two think you're doing? Trading at the farmers' market or something? I'm a *human,* Pauly-the-Pig. Get out of here, Pauly."

"No, wait," he says. "I want to show you something, Lilly. Come here."

"I don't want another poem. They make me ill."

"Hey, I said I was a poet. I never said I was a *gifted* poet. Anyway, it's not a poem. It's something better, even."

"I don't want *that,* either. I *especially* don't want that. And if you try to show it to me again, I'll call the Reverend."

"It's not that either," Pauly says, exasperated.

I'm starting to get a little embarrassed. "Maybe I should go."

"No, you absolutely shouldn't," she says to me.

Pauly. "Just come to the window, Lilly."

Lilly. "Ignore him, Oakley."

Me. "How can you ignore Pauly? How can anyone ignore Pauly?"

Lilly. "Easy."

Pauly. "Not anymore, it ain't. I'm going to be unignorable. C'mere."

Lilly sighs, turns up the sound on the TV with the remote.

"Well, I'm going to go look," I say. She shrugs.

When I'm almost to the window and Pauly is reaching down into his pants, the sound of the Reverend's car on the gravel driveway pulls Pauly's attention like a scared deer listening to the wind. And like a deer, he is gone in an instant, into the trees and out of sight.

"He's been getting weirder and weirder since I told him about the college," Lilly says, shaking her head at the silent-again television.

Lilly #50

Girl sits with boy but doesn't never
really talk
Like her mouth's been all taped
and stuffed
with a sock

she'll think of him well though
when he's outlined
in chalk
or when some body's brain cells
are splashed
on a rock

—by paulY

"Think she'll like it?" he asks me.

I don't know what to say. Everybody always says that, but here I am totally true about it. I have no idea what to tell him.

"You mean, the poem?"

"No, stupid, I know she's going to like the poem. It's my best work."

In that case, he must mean the other thing.

"So, what do you think?"

What I think is, I think I might fall down right here, my knees are so weak.

"I think, get that away from me, Pauly, that's what I think."

"Ah, ya big baby. It's not gonna hurt you. Look, she's cocked and locked here, so she looks ready to fire, but she won't."

She being the Colt.

"I thought Colt 45 was a drink," I say as I take a few steps backwards, toward the cider press.

Pauly follows me, chuckling. "You're funny, Oak. Here, check it out."

As if I could *avoid* checking it out. It was the same shape as the state of Texas, with the barrel pointing north, the hammer pointing west, the handle sticking down into Mexico's side, and the shooter's knuckles scraping along from Louisiana to Oklahoma.

Nearly as big as Texas too. When skinny old Pauly waved the thing around, it pulled his arm along like he wasn't in charge of it at all.

"That's okay," I say. "I can see it fine."

"You can't see it. You gotta *feel* it, is the thing, Oakley."

He grabs my wrist and works the monster into my palm. My hand closes around it, and it nearly pulls me to the ground.

"She's gonna go 'wow,' " Pauly says.

"She's gonna go *something,* " I say. I can feel my free hand shaking as I examine the Colt up close.

But Pauly is right about this: it's unignorable.

It's like, every line is in place. Every straight is straight, every curve is schwoop; it's cool to the touch, but feels so comfortable in the fleshy innermost of the palm that you feel as if it knows what it's doing, and it probably belongs there. The barrel is polished blue gray, almost the same color as the late-afternoon light behind the hill, and the brilliant stainless steel body catches every chip of that light and forces you to pay close attention.

Automatically, like a five-year-old, I raise it up, close one eye, and point it. At an apple tree. At a squirrel.

"Where'd you get it?" I ask.

"Really want to know?"

I look up at my friend's face, to see whether in fact I do. He smiles crookedly. I don't.

"Borrowed it from the Rev's collection that he doesn't want nobody to know about. He knows *I* know, though."

I knew I didn't want to know.

"She's leaving because of me, because I'm boring her," Pauly says.

I aim at the little rusted rooster twisting on top of the cider press house. "Pauly, you are many things—in fact, you're *most* things I can think of to call somebody—but one thing you could never be is boring."

"Well, *we* know that, but I think Lilly is bored with me, and that's why she's leaving Whitechurch."

"She's leaving Whitechurch to go to school. If the university was here, she wouldn't be leaving."

"That's just an excuse," he says.

Lilly is where she's supposed to be. Pauly told her to meet him. I'm not where I'm supposed to be. I'm not supposed to be here at all. But when Lilly told me he wanted her to meet him at our spot above the prison yard, I decided I should be here. It's Wednesday afternoon, and as we wait for Pauly, we listen to the fife-and-drum-and-bagpipe corps. They've been getting better. They've got "Loch Lomond" pretty well nailed.

But they're not supposed to be here. It's not Thursday.

"Sounds so pretty," Lilly says. "How come you guys never told me about this before? This is sweet."

I nod. She looks nervous, no matter what she says.

"Did he tell you what he wanted you up here for?"

"Said he wants to show me something. But he's always saying that. To tell you the truth, he hasn't really shown me anything in a long time."

I let out a low, steady whistle, the kind that everybody knows means "Oh, boy."

"Well, what can I say, Oakley? You understand, I know you do. There's nothing wrong with what I'm doing."

Of course I understand. The Lilly-Pauly relationship was always the type of thing that practically brought "Booooo" calls from the whole town. The Reverend, for one, would carry her on his back to Boston, with all her luggage, to get her away from him.

"He'll be okay," I say, and I have never said a more outrageous thing. "In fact, you probably don't even have to wait for him now. I'll talk to him. He'll be—"

"What the hell are *they* doing down there," Pauly says, popping up behind us quiet as a catamount. He walks right on past us and points down at the prison yard with the Colt.

"My God, Pauly!" Lilly gasps. We both jump to our feet. "What is that?"

"They are not supposed to be there," he insists. "This isn't Thursday. Is it? Oakley, is this Thursday?"

I start to answer, but he cuts me off.

"And *you're* not supposed to be here, either. This

was supposed to be a special moment between me and my girl."

He is gesturing at me with it now. But he doesn't mean anything by it.

"I can't be your girl anymore, Pauly. I'm not that."

It is my turn to gasp. "Do you *see* what he's holding, Lillian? Maybe you could save this conversation—"

"I'm very worried about you leaving," he says. "You need me, Lilly, we all know that."

Lilly shakes her head.

"Listen," I say. "She's not even leaving for months yet. Why don't we save all this, okay? We have the spring and the summer still and it'll be the same . . . it'll be better, even, than all the others. Then, next year when Pauly and me graduate, we'll come down and join you and everything will be back—"

"You need me, Lilly," he repeats. "We all know that. You're just a little bored with things right now, you want a little—"

"Pauly," she says calmly, but not without a little tremor. "Pauly . . ." She doesn't seem to know how to finish.

Pauly wheels around to face the small figures down in the prison yard again. He's staring. I hear the distinctive *click-click* of the hammer pulling back.

"Cocked, Pauly, huh?" I say. "Locked?"

He pauses for a long time. He nods. "Cocked and locked."

Pauly doesn't want to hurt anybody. I know Pauly

doesn't want to hurt anybody. Lilly knows it too. We're probably the two people in town who know. In the fall, there'll only be one.

He turns back to face us, and as he does he aims straight up into the cloudless azure blue of the sky. The Colt blends with it, with the blue, as if it were a siphon, drinking blue down out of the air, down through the polished blue muzzle, through the faded blue arm of Pauly's old fleece-lined denim jacket, and into the blue body of pale Paul himself. Feeding into him, so much bigger than him.

"Do you see this?" he asks her. "Don't you *see* this, Lilly?"

"I do," she says. "Does it lead us to something, Pauly?"

We all wait on that. Lilly and I wait more out of courtesy than fear, to give him a chance to withdraw with dignity.

"You need me" is all he can manage.

With that, Lilly turns and walks away, leaving Paul with his hand still stuck in the air. He stares at her back for an awfully long time.

I don't turn to watch Lilly leave, because I don't stop watching Pauly. But I can see by the draining of his face when she has cleared out of sight.

"You're not leaving me, though, are you, Oakley?" he asks, lowering the Colt finally.

"Of course I'm not leaving you."

He turns back toward the prison and sits down cross-legged in the dirt.

I sit next to him. "Somebody would notice," I remind him. "And it wouldn't be a good notice."

Pauly finally smiles. He leans a shoulder into me, tipping me over onto the ground.

"Ah, we didn't need her anyway, did we, Oak?"

"Nah," I say, propping up on one elbow. "Let her fly."

"Let her fly," he says.

Then Pauly puts the nozzle of the Colt in his mouth. He has to open his jaws all the way to fit the thing in there.

I stay frozen to the ground. While I do, and while Pauly remains likewise still, he rolls just his eyes in my direction. When he's had a good look at my stricken face, the smile comes back to him again. He looks like a skeleton with the pistol in his teeth.

"Almost looked sick there, buddy," he says as he pulls it out.

"Almost was," I say.

"That's good," he says. "That's good." He stands and offers me a hand. "We can go home now," he says.

When he's got me halfway to my feet, he drops me. I'm on the seat of my pants. He comes right up close to me.

"Put this in your mouth," he says coolly.

I say nothing. I feel the blood-warmth run out of my face like a flushing toilet. The big hole at the tip of the Colt is now pressed like a cold mouth against mine.

"Go ahead now, Oakley. Do what I tell you."

I open up, and my friend doesn't hesitate before easing the barrel in, the sight scraping along the roof of my mouth. Pauly pulls back on the hammer, and it sounds like the mechanism is clacking and clacking, tumbling like the lock on a gigantic steel vault.

"What does it taste like?" he asks. "It tastes blue, don't you think?"

Of course I can't answer.

"Not nervous, are you? Oak? Of course not. Cocked and locked, right?"

There is another click.

"Cocked . . . unlocked," he says, grinning. "Did I tell you how sensitive the Colt 45 semiautomatic is? I didn't? Oh, let me, then. When it's cocked and un-locked, this piece will fire if you *tell* it to fire."

There is nothing for me to do, then, except keep on looking up into Pauly's tired, watery eyes. So I keep on. Until finally I see, in there, where *my* Pauly is, and he looks back at me.

He blinks away some of the glaze.

Slowly, gingerly, I back off. *Remove* myself from the gun.

He points it into the dirt and uncocks it.

"You're my friend, Oakley," he says.

"I am," I say.

He raises the Colt again, points it in my face. "If I tell you to put this back in your mouth once more, are you still my friend?"

I open my mouth as wide as I can.

Pauly puts the gun in my hand, and he starts to cry.
"I'm going to write you a poem," he says. *"Oakley #1."*

I tug on his jacket and start him down the hill.
"You do and I'll shoot ya," I say.

CHRIS LYNCH is a popular and acclaimed author of young adult fiction. His novels *Shadow Boxer, Iceman, Gypsy Davey,* and *Slot Machine* were all selected as American Library Association Best Books for Young Adults. He is also the author of *Political Timber,* the Blue-Eyed Son trilogy, and the He-Man Women Haters Club series. He is currently writing a collection of stories titled *Whitechurch* that will feature the same town and characters as "Cocked & Locked."

"My own experience with guns is not extensive," Chris Lynch says, "although I did go out in the woods with a friend and his dad to shoot, and I did find an old rusted handgun on my way home from school in fifth grade. But the story means more to me as an extension of something I address frequently, especially in my shorter work: violence, and sexuality, and domination, and the potent mixing of the three in the adolescent male psyche."

HUNTING BEAR

by Kevin McColley

"The reason I come to you," Jack Taylor explained, "is because I know your father."

Gerry Lind glanced at the man sitting across the table from him, at his tailored shirt, at his expensive brown leather jacket. "I'm not my father."

"But you worked with him, right?"

"Sure."

"And you know the forest, right?"

"This part of it."

"That's why I come to you."

Gerry picked at his meal. They were sitting in Roscoe's on the Lake, a restaurant Gerry walked by every day during the school year without ever going inside. He was eating grilled duck breast wrapped in its own skin. It had cost Mr. Taylor thirty dollars. "There's no bear left in this part of Minnesota."

Mr. Taylor grunted and sipped his wine. "I used to

hunt here with your father all the time. There was always bear then. He'd jump at this opportunity."

Anger flashed in Gerry's chest. A year before, his father had taken a group of Japanese businessmen on an out-of-season hunt for black bear—they ground up the gallbladders for aphrodisiacs, love dust. One of the businessmen had actually been an agent with the Department of Natural Resources. *John Lind, you have the right to remain silent. Anything you say can and will be used against you in a court of law. You have the right to an attorney. . . .* But the attorney hadn't done much good. Three to five, they'd given him.

Gerry swallowed his anger down. He didn't like thinking about his father. "He wouldn't jump now, even if he could. There's no bear left."

A grin crawled like a worm across Mr. Taylor's face. "You ever hunted elk, Gerry?"

"I've always wanted to."

"In the Bighorns in Wyoming, right? With a Mannlicher Luxus S Magnum?"

Gerry and the old man, his grandfather, had always talked about a trip to the Bighorns. It was a dream they'd never been able to afford. "How did you know that?"

"Your father used to tell me about it. What's a Mannlicher run nowadays?"

Gerry shrugged. "They're expensive. About three grand."

"Expense is all relative. What's expensive to you, for

example, would not be expensive to me." Mr. Taylor
finished his meal and lit a cigarette. "Money," he said,
"can do anything. It can make people do anything."
He pointed out the patio door at the back of the restaurant toward Pine Lake. A pretty woman in shorts
and a T-shirt was climbing over a speedboat's gunwale
onto one of the restaurant's docks. "I can make that
woman strip off her clothes and cackle like a chicken
with the money I have in my pocket right now. Do
you believe that?"

Gerry didn't know if he believed it or not. Everybody has a price, a line they won't cross. "Money can't
make bears appear in the woods."

Mr. Taylor sucked on the cigarette and blew a
smoke plume into the air. "I'll pay you three grand for
a bear. Half now, and half when we bag it."

The last of the duck caught in Gerry's throat.
"What?"

"Three and a half," Mr. Taylor said. "Make it four
to cover expenses."

Gerry chased the duck down with a swallow of
Coke he was too dazzled to taste. Four grand for a bear
meant three grand he'd have for a Mannlicher, and a
Mannlicher was sweet, so sweet. Walnut, hand-check-
ered stock, .30/06 caliber, and a bolt action as smooth
as butter—one of the finest rifles in the world. And the
extra grand would cover a trip to the Bighorns.

"I'd like to get there before I die," the old man
always said, and his eyes always misted over when he

said it. Gerry had lived with him since they'd arrested
his father, had eaten his food, had spent his money,
had unbalanced a life that had taken the old man
seventy-two years to balance. The eerie, lonely call of a
bull elk echoed in Gerry's mind. He owed the old man
something. But there were no bear.

He thought about it, then nodded. For four grand,
he'd find a bear. "What kind of a rifle do you use?" he
asked.

Mr. Taylor smiled. "A Kreighoff over and under
with a side-by-side box lock. Three seventy-five Holland and Holland caliber."

"Nice gun."

"It ought to be. It cost me fourteen grand." He
drew on his cigarette. "You?"

"My grandfather's old Winchester Ranger."

Mr. Taylor shrugged. "Not a bad gun, for the price.
Four hundred bucks or so, isn't it?"

The woman from the dock came through the patio
door. Gerry imagined her squatting naked on the floor
and flapping her arms like wings, money from Mr.
Taylor's thick wallet cascading down upon her. The
Mannlicher and the trip to the Bighorns, the old man,
floated again through his mind. He imagined himself
squatting and flapping beside her.

Mr. Taylor pulled a checkbook out of his jacket
pocket and began writing in it. "I have to fly to Hous-
ton first on some business. Should I meet you here for
breakfast on Sunday?"

Six days, Gerry thought. Could he find a bear in six days? "Bears move more at dusk. You better meet me here for supper."

"Fine." Mr. Taylor handed Gerry the check.

Gerry studied it. Two grand, he thought, and I haven't done anything yet. "Why, Mr. Taylor? Why are you spending four grand to hunt a bear here when you could hunt one somewhere else for the price of a license?"

Mr. Taylor put his checkbook away. "Let's just say I like to get people to do what I want them to do." He smiled at the woman as she sat at the table beside them. She smiled back. "That's the real hunting, isn't it?"

Gerry searched in the forest all the places where black bear were likely to be—the berry patches, the clearing edges, the game trails, the tall stands of red pine, white pine, and birch. He found nothing—no prints, no territory markings, no dens, no scat, no nothing. He found deer, he found moose, he found raccoons, he even found a wolf kill ten miles north of Pine Lake. He found no bear.

One day, two days, three days. He came home on the evening of the fourth day desperate enough to check the yellow pages.

"What do you expect to find?" he muttered as he slapped the book shut. "Do bears advertise?"

He fixed supper for himself and the old man—venison, potatoes, and carrots thrown into a pressure cooker with a splash of soy sauce and red wine vinegar—then while it cooked, went out on the porch where the old man was sitting, a kerosene lantern on the table beside him hissing softly. Gerry sat beside him and studied the old, scarred Winchester leaning in the corner, the gentle brown of its stock and the bluing of its barrel softly diffusing the light. He'd taken a lot of deer with that rifle, and a bear once. But it didn't look good beside the Mannlicher filling his mind, and to think about it and the Kreighoff together was only embarrassing.

Not a bad gun, Mr. Taylor had said, *for the price.*

The old man was tall and lean with a brilliant shock of white hair and a walrus mustache that glowed in the light. He sat with his legs stretched out before him, reading a copy of *Moby-Dick.* "The whale in this is one tough mother," he said. "Too bad he's white. I bet all the other whales teased him."

Gerry studied the old man's heavily lined cheeks, then looked again at the Winchester. *One last trip,* he thought. He sighed. "Sure."

"Trouble?" the old man asked. "A sigh like that usually means trouble."

Gerry turned from the Winchester to the growing darkness. The house had been built by the old man in the sixties, with no electricity or running water. The outhouse at the edge of the trees leaned slightly toward the sunset, as if it were frightened of the night.

"You still think about that trip to the Bighorns?" he asked.

The old man looked up. "Sometimes."

A loon called from Pine Lake, beyond the trees. The old man closed his book and set it on the table beside the lantern. "Talk about it," he said.

"Talk about what?"

"About whatever's got you so fidgety. Is it your dad?"

Gerry shrugged. "He's part of it."

"Your dad got a little mixed up. He started to think that he could buy what would make him happy, and he started looking for ways that would let him do the buying. He's not happy, Gerry."

"I know."

Gerry looked at the Winchester again and imagined the Mannlicher beside it. He imagined tramping through a forest in the Bighorns with the old man a step behind him. The trees opened onto a rolling green meadow, and the peaks were a white-tipped ring around it, and in the distance the dark, graceful, unbelievably beautiful form of a bull elk moved slowly; it floated like a dream. Its head went back, and it bellowed. The old man's breath came cloudy in the crisp fall air as he rested his hand on Gerry's shoulder and smiled.

The old man stretched in his chair and watched the night. "It said in the paper this afternoon that there's a circus coming to Oleander. Maybe you should find yourself a pretty girl and take her. Take your mind off your troubles."

"Do you suppose it'll have a bear act?" Gerry asked.

Oleander was a cluster of houses on the county road thirty miles into the forest east of Pine Lake. Gerry borrowed the old man's pickup and drove over on Saturday afternoon. The circus had been set up on the west side of town—a single blue-and-white tent propped up by four poles, one at each corner, and a half dozen semitrailers with tigers and clowns painted on their sides. He parked the pickup on the shoulder and walked toward the ticket booth, a white-painted plywood and chicken-wire box with the words THE KIWALSKI FAMILY CIRCUS: ADULTS $5.00, CHILDREN $2.50 painted in red letters on a sign above it. He didn't see any bears.

He bought his ticket and went inside. Spotlights hanging from each of the poles lit the interior. It held only one ring, with a flap in the back opening onto the evening and a long row of old wooden bleachers opposite it. Gerry sat high in the back in the canvas shadows and watched a bald dwarf work the crowd, selling peanuts and cotton candy. Half the kids were taller than the dwarf, and the look on his face said he resented it.

Five minutes passed. Something coughed weakly behind the tent, and Gerry sat up straight. He saw nothing beyond the flap but shadows. Could it have been a bear?

A man in a black top hat and high leather boots and carrying a megaphone stepped through the flap and into the ring. His potbelly cast a shadow over his belt. "Ladies and gentlemen, boys and girls, welcome to the greatest show on Earth!"

The children clapped wildly, but the adults seemed to have their doubts about his statement. The ringmaster held open the flap and a woman standing on a horse galloped into the ring, her long, dark hair lifting and falling. A clown followed the horse around with a scoop shovel, cleaning up its mess. He didn't even try to be funny. The children laughed anyway.

A high-wire act followed the horse, then a sleepy elephant. After it took a couple of turns, an old male lion trudged into the ring and perched on a stool as the ringmaster cracked a whip. When it roared, Gerry knew where the weak cough had come from—a real roar seemed too much for a lion this old to muster. Gerry saw that trip to the Bighorns flutter away like a butterfly.

He watched the clown and the dwarf ride around in a little red truck and halfheartedly slap each other with hot-water bottles before he decided to leave. He climbed down the bleachers as the little red truck drove outside through the flap. The dwarf entered again with a bear. Gerry sat on the bottom bleacher, suddenly interested.

The dwarf tossed the bear a ball. The bear caught it,

set it down, and kicked it back. It caromed off to the right, bouncing off the ring, and the dwarf had to chase it down. Except for a strange white blaze on its chest, the bear looked just like a black. It could pass for a black, anyway, and that was all Gerry cared about. He stood and walked outside.

The air was clear, the stars brilliant above the forest darkness. Gerry walked around to the back. The clown was standing to the side of the flap, smoking cigarettes with the woman who had stood on the horse. Her long, dark hair—a wig—was sitting on a wooden crate beside her. Her real hair was gray. She could have been eighty.

"I want to talk to the ringmaster," Gerry said to their heavy, silent stares.

The clown crushed out his cigarette. "He'll be out in a minute."

The bear rode out of the tent on a little bike with training wheels. The voice of the ringmaster announced a clown act. The clown swore, sighed, and trudged back inside. The woman studied Gerry as she finished her cigarette, then disappeared into the darkness. The bear pedaled in a circle happily.

The ringmaster came out a minute later. He set his hat on the crate and ran his fingers through his thinning hair. "The name is Maurice Kiwalski. Happy said you wanted to see me."

"Gerry Lind. I want to buy your bear."

Maurice laughed and ran his hands over his belly. "What for?"

"That's my business. Five hundred bucks." Maurice laughed again. "A thousand."

Maurice quit laughing. He studied Gerry, then studied the bear as it rode the bike into and out of the light falling through the flap. "He isn't much good. He has to use training wheels. You saw him kick the ball, didn't you? He kicks like a sissy."

"Do you want to sell him, or not?"

Maurice ran his fingers through his hair. From within the tent came the wet slap of a hot-water bottle. "I can't sell him—as bad as he is, he's one of our best acts."

"All right." Gerry started to walk away.

"Wait a minute. That doesn't mean I don't want to sell you a bear."

Gerry stopped. The bear rode around and around, ringing the bicycle bell and chortling with glee. Maurice took Gerry's arm. "Come with me."

He led Gerry into the cluster of trailers. The night felt thicker between them, and a little cooler. Maurice nodded at a catwalk leading up into a door opening onto darkness.

"In there," he said.

"You first."

Gerry followed Maurice up the catwalk, its boards bowing with each step. Maurice turned on a light just as Gerry stepped inside. Crates were everywhere; a dusty picture of Emmett Kelly hung loosely on the wall. The old lion lay in a cage by the door, snoring loudly and probably dreaming of Africa. In the back corner against the wall stood a second cage, and in the cage was a bear.

Maurice led Gerry to the back. The bear was black with a tan muzzle and a white crescent on its chest. Its head was large and round, almost the size of a basketball, and its little round ears were set far back from its face. Its muzzle broke into a grin as its tongue came out to lick the end of its nose.

"Gruhnnk," it said.

"She's too old for the act," Maurice explained. "Her joints are getting stiff, and she can't see to catch the ball."

Gerry squatted and rested his hand on the cage. The bear licked his fingers. "What kind of a bear is this?"

"An Asian sun bear, the finest circus bears in the world."

"What's she weigh? Two fifty?"

"About."

"She's pretty small."

"You said you wanted a bear. You didn't say what size. You want her or not?"

She licked Gerry's fingers again. No, he didn't want her. Though he had seen white blazes on black bears before, he had never seen one like this—it was as if her chest had broken into a grin. But he didn't have much of a choice—Mr. Taylor would be waiting at Roscoe's the next evening. "Yeah, I want her."

She grunted deep in her chest and rolled onto her

back. Maurice opened the cage door and scratched her belly. "She wants you to scratch her when she does that. Go ahead, try it."

"I don't want to try it."

"Don't worry, she won't bite."

Gerry scratched her belly. It was warm, almost hot, and the fur was thick, soft, and shiny. She sighed deeply and closed her eyes. She'd make a nice rug.

"We agreed on a thousand dollars," Gerry said. That was the trip to the Bighorns, but with hard work and a lot of smiling he figured he could wheedle an extra thousand out of Mr. Taylor. Everything would fall into place.

"Twelve hundred will include the cage."

"I don't need the cage."

"What are you going to do with her?"

I'm going to let someone shoot her, Gerry thought. "A pet."

Maurice reached down to scratch the bear's ears. He smiled as she grunted happily. "She'll make a good one. Old Daisy is as gentle as a kitten."

"I thought you were supposed to name bears tough names, like Bruno or Griz."

"Daisy's a lady," Maurice said.

Maurice gave Gerry a collar, a leash, and feeding instructions—she liked red meat, corn, and cranberries. "You have to mash it all together," he said. "Her teeth are getting bad."

"Cranberries?" Gerry asked.

Maurice shrugged. "Who can understand the taste of a bear? Use cranberry sauce—she chokes on the real thing. And look out for loud noises. They scare her."

She'll only hear one, Gerry thought—*a Kreighoff over and under going* boom. "I will."

He tried to get Daisy to sit in the pickup bed, but she insisted on squeezing into the cab beside him. She had to sit sideways, her rump against the door and her round, basketball head against Gerry's cheek like a lover's. She licked his ear.

Gerry brushed her away. "Knock it off, will you?" He didn't want to get this intimate with an animal that would be dead within twenty-four hours. *Think about that trip to the Bighorns,* he thought. *Think about that Mannlicher. Think about the old man smiling in a mountain meadow.* Daisy kept licking.

He put her in the garage when he got home, but she whined so loudly he worried she'd wake up the old man. She spent the night in his bedroom, on the bed, with Gerry on the floor in a sleeping bag. At the grocery store in the morning he bought ten dollars' worth of hamburger, frozen corn, and cranberry sauce.

While the old man was taking his morning walk, Gerry loaded the food and a large pan into a backpack. He hauled it out to the pickup bed, went up to his bedroom, and led Daisy outside. She insisted on riding in the cab and licking his ear.

"Gruhnnk," she said.

Gerry followed an old forest service road north into

the woods, stopping ten miles in at the little bridge
spanning Ferrel Stream, a narrow brook that emptied
into Pine Lake. He parked, got out of the cab, and
slung the pack over his shoulders. Daisy watched him
with big, brown eyes. He didn't look at her. She'd be
dead by nightfall.

As he walked around to the passenger door, tires
ground on gravel. He looked up to see a man in tight
shorts bicycle around the curve just beyond the bridge.
The bicycle had one of those children's bells on the
handlebars, and the man smiled as he rang it.

Gerry waved and smiled and felt his chest tighten as
he tried to block the man's view of the cab. After the
bike had gone by and disappeared into the trees, Gerry
heaved a sigh and opened the passenger door. Too
much was riding on this to have some skinny guy in
tight shorts screw it up.

"Come on," he said. Daisy lumbered out of the cab,
stretched, and rolled belly-up in the brush. "None of
that, now. This is business."

She wouldn't move. He scratched her, and she
sighed contentedly. Her belly was as warm as it had
been the night before, the crescent as much of a grin.
She was old, but she still had a lot of life burning in
her. Gerry had to look away. A sick feeling crawled
through his stomach.

Think about that trip to the Bighorns, he reminded
himself. *Think about that Mannlicher. Think about the
old man smiling in a mountain meadow.*

"*Gruhnnk,*" Daisy said.

He led her by the leash up the brook and deep into the trees, the sunlight so filtered that all was shadow. Daisy walked delicately—the roughest thing her paws had probably ever touched was a bicycle pedal. Gerry led her slowly eastward for half a mile to a clearing ringed with raspberry bushes. He slipped off the pack and took out the pan. Into it he emptied the hamburger, corn, and cranberries. Daisy stared at it, then rolled on her back.

"You're making this hard," Gerry said.

She sighed.

He took off her collar, then scratched her. *She's not just a trophy,* he found himself thinking, and he had to shake his head to clear the thought away. He thought instead of the trip to the Bighorns, the Mannlicher, and the old man smiling in a mountain meadow, but that other thought kept sneaking in. He had to get away from her to where he could think clearly, to where he wouldn't have to feel the heat of her on his hand, to where he wouldn't have to look into her eyes.

"Stay," he ordered her. *Is* stay *a command you can use with a bear? Do bears have commands?*

"Gruhnnk," she answered.

He walked out of the clearing. Daisy whined. As the clearing faded into the trees the whine grew into a cry, then a tremendous crash in the underbrush. He turned. She jogged up beside him and licked his hand.

"No, Daisy. Stay." He took two steps toward the pickup. So did she. He took two more. So did she.

Finally, Gerry sighed and walked back to the clearing. Daisy jogged happily after him. "I'll stay with you for a little while," he said, "but then I have to go. I have to meet Jack Taylor at Roscoe's tonight, before . . ." The words caught on the lump in his throat. *Before we shoot you. Before you die.*

He sat. She laid her big, black head in his lap, looked up at him, and grunted with satisfaction. Her little round ears twitched in the sunlight.

A trip to the Bighorns, Gerry thought. *A Mannlicher. The old man smiling.*

She rolled on her back, and he scratched her stomach. Gerry kept scratching until her eyes closed and she began to snore. He stood quietly, careful not to wake her. He followed the stream back to the pickup.

Jack Taylor was already eating by the time Gerry reached Roscoe's. On his plate lay a thick T-bone steak, a baked potato, and a pile of steaming green beans. A half-empty wine glass sat in front of him, with a half-empty bottle of Cabernet Sauvignon beside it.

"I like to eat plenty before a hunt," he said. "Do you have something for me?"

"Maybe." Gerry sat. "But it took a lot of work."

Mr. Taylor swallowed. "You want more money. How much? Five hundred?"

"A thousand would be better."

Mr. Taylor sighed. "If your father and I weren't friends . . ."

"Don't talk about my father." *Your dad got a little mixed up,* the old man had said. Gerry didn't want to be reminded of it. Like father, like son.

"If your father and I weren't friends," Mr. Taylor repeated, "I'd tell you to jump in the lake. But we're friends. And it's only a thousand." He cut loose a big chunk of steak and stuffed it into his mouth. "I knew you were lying about there being no bear. You were saving them for those Japanese businessmen, weren't you?"

"Yeah," Gerry said.

"But they didn't offer five grand, did they?"

"No, they didn't."

Mr. Taylor smiled and drained his wine. "Eat, and let's get out of here."

Gerry ordered a walleye fillet and a plate of hash browned potatoes. He stared out at the water. *In a few minutes,* he thought, *Jack Taylor and I will be heading out to find Daisy. In a few minutes, a three-hundred-seventy-five-caliber Holland and Holland bullet will leave the barrel of a fourteen-thousand-dollar Kreighoff and slam into her chest. In a few minutes,* he thought, *right and wrong and good and bad and being a little mixed up won't make any difference. It'll be done.*

He could only pick at his meal. Everyone has a price.

Gerry parked on the side of the road just before the Ferrel Stream bridge. A sick feeling rose in his throat, a sick feeling born of what he was about to do, born of what he had done. Daisy was about to die.

A trip to the Bighorns, he thought. *A Mannlicher. A smile on the old man's face.*

Everyone has a price.

He shut off the engine and turned in his seat toward Mr. Taylor. "Let's call this off. You can keep your money. I spent some of the advance, but I'll pay you back."

Mr. Taylor dug a cartridge out of his breast pocket and sighed. "What'll it take? Another thousand?"

"I don't want your money."

"You're not getting out of this. If you don't guide, I'll turn you in for poaching."

"I'll talk. You'll go in with me."

Mr. Taylor grinned. "I can buy every high-priced lawyer between here and Los Angeles. If you talk, those lawyers will have the judge's head spinning so fast that he'll be apologizing to me. And I'll buy that judge and see that you're locked away with your father. How does two to five years in the state penitentiary sound? How about five to eight?"

"You can't do that."

"Yeah?" He smiled. "Are you going to guide for me or not?"

Gerry stared out of the window. None of those rich Japanese businessmen had gone to jail—only his father had.

"I'll be nice and let you keep the money," Mr. Taylor said, "but first you have to find me a bear."

Gerry watched him climb out of the cab and lift the Kreighoff's shiny, black leather case out of the pickup bed. He opened the case to reveal the rifle, its nickel-plated receiver and oiled German stock glowing red in the dying sun.

"You coming?" Mr. Taylor asked.

Gerry opened the door. *Everyone has a price,* he thought again. "I'm coming."

He took the Winchester out of the pickup bed, the stock scarred with years, the barrel slick in its protective oil film. He loaded five cartridges into the magazine and wondered what would become of them.

"Lead on," Mr. Taylor said.

Gerry led him upstream, his ears listening for any sound of Daisy, his eyes open for any flash of shadow. His finger ached as it gripped the trigger guard. The woods were warm and heavy with the evening. The mosquitoes danced.

"Look at this, Gerry." Mr. Taylor squatted, the Kreighoff cradled in his arm, his fingertips passing gently over the ground. "Bear prints."

"I saw them."

"And boot prints."

"They belong to me. I put out food up ahead to attract her."

Mr. Taylor looked up. "Her? How do you know it's a her?"

"I just know."

Mr. Taylor grinned. The salty, sweaty smells of wine

and excitement rolled up from him, as thick in the
air as the dusk. "A born tracker, just like your
father."

Daisy's footprints littered the clearing. The food
pan was empty and the raspberry bushes ravaged. Mr.
Taylor tapped the pan with the toe of his boot. "What
did you use to bait her?"

"Hamburger, corn, and cranberries."

"Did you get that recipe from your father?"

"Yeah."

"He's a good man—he was just unlucky enough to
get caught. Find her."

Gerry dropped to his haunches and studied the
prints. Maybe he could lead Mr. Taylor away from her.
Maybe, if he worked at it, they would never find her at
all.

He stood and pointed with the muzzle of the Winchester upstream. "She went that way."

"Lead on."

Gerry did. Mr. Taylor followed him fifty feet, then
stopped. "There's no prints."

"Bears have tender feet. She would have circled
around to avoid the rocks."

The forest was silent as the sun settled lower, the air
gray with the dusk. Suddenly, something grunted and
crashed in the brush. Gerry's hopes tumbled as a big,
black shadow broke free from a stand of paper birch
thirty yards ahead. Daisy came at them, galloping the
way a bear does, with her head down and snaking

from side to side, her body moving amazingly fast. She grunted happily.

"She's charging!" Mr. Taylor's Kreighoff came up in a smooth, graceful sweep. "I've got her!"

Gerry dropped to avoid the muzzle, but when something rose inside him, he rose with it. His shoulder caught the barrel, forcing it up to point at the trees.

The explosion was tremendous, and in its ringing silence Gerry saw Daisy pull up short, saw her eyes go wide, saw her bolt into the trees. Mr. Taylor pushed him aside and set himself for a second shot. It tore through the brush above her shoulder. She disappeared into the shadows. Gerry smiled.

The first thing he heard when the explosion quit echoing was Mr. Taylor cursing. "What's the matter with you, kid?"

"I spooked." Gerry shook the ringing from his head. "I've never been charged by a bear before."

Mr. Taylor reloaded the Kreighoff with two big, ugly cartridges. "Your father wouldn't have spooked. He wouldn't have ruined my shot!"

"I'm not my father."

"Get after her! That's what I'm paying you for!"

Gerry jogged into the brush. The prints were heavy and deep, the moldering leaves kicked back as she had dashed away. He followed her trail fifty yards with Mr. Taylor sweating and panting and cursing behind him. Beside a tangled downfall Daisy had broken back toward the clearing. Gerry worked deeper into the trees.

Mr. Taylor stopped. "You idiot! She went the other way!"

Gerry ambled back to where he was standing. He had bought her a second or two. Would a second or two be enough?

"I want this one," Mr. Taylor said. "No bear makes a fool out of me."

"This one seems to be doing a pretty good job of it."

"We'll see if you'll be making such smart remarks in prison. You better find me that bear."

The prints led back to the clearing and across it, then downstream in a wide, panicky lope. They were too clear now for Gerry to lead Mr. Taylor astray. When they were an eighth of a mile from the road, something screamed.

"That sounded human to me," Mr. Taylor said.

The scream came again. Gerry broke into a jog, stumbling over roots, dizzy with confusion. He saw in his mind Daisy standing over a mangled body with her teeth bared, red and dripping. She didn't have it in her to attack anyone, did she? But bears are bears, and she was frightened. And she'd been betrayed.

Another scream echoed. It was close, not more than fifty yards away. The trees thinned, and Gerry stumbled onto the forest service road. The bicyclist Gerry had seen the day before was sprinting south toward town, the shiny fabric of his shorts flashing in the last of the sun. Mr. Taylor scanned the trees with the Kreighoff held across his chest.

Daisy's prints burst out of the forest beside the bridge. They skidded to a stop in the dirt, then turned north. Gerry followed them toward the curve in the road. Suddenly, he stopped.

There was one large set of prints in the center of the road with none ahead of it. They were there, and then they were gone. Daisy was there, and then she was gone. Gerry rubbed his eyes. It didn't make any sense.

"Where'd she go?" Mr. Taylor demanded. "Back into the woods?"

"No. She just . . . she just isn't here anymore."

Mr. Taylor stared at the prints. "Bears don't just disappear."

"Then you explain it."

Mr. Taylor cradled the Kreighoff in the crook of his arm and knelt. He ran his fingers over the prints. He looked up, then pointed. "There she is!"

Just around the curve, Daisy's furry, black head moved smoothly above the brush. Mr. Taylor stood and raised the Kreighoff, then cursed and lowered the rifle when she disappeared behind the trees. He sprinted toward the curve.

No, Gerry thought. *No. Bighorns or no Bighorns, Mannlicher or no Mannlicher, prison or no prison, I can't let this happen. I owe the old man, but I don't owe him this. I can't owe him this.*

He dove for Mr. Taylor's boots, but his hands only

caught one heel and the man hardly stumbled. Mr. Taylor ran to the curve with Gerry sucking on road dirt and cursing. Gerry scrambled to his feet and ran after him. Mr. Taylor stopped at the curve, raised the rifle, and aimed.

"No!" Gerry shouted.

Mr. Taylor's mouth dropped open. The Kreighoff dropped and hung loosely at his side. The only sound was the hum of the insects, was the occasional call of a bird.

"I don't believe it," Mr. Taylor said.

Gerry reached the curve. Daisy was a hundred yards away and moving fast. She was sitting on a bicycle, her big, black rump overhanging the seat, her furry legs pumping away. Stones spit up from the tires.

Mr. Taylor let the Kreighoff fall to the ground; he rubbed his eyes. "Do you see that?"

"I see it," Gerry said.

"No," Mr. Taylor said, "do you *see* that?"

Daisy's little round ears twitched as she rang the bell on the handlebar. *"Gruhnnk,"* she said as she disappeared around a curve in the road.

Mr. Taylor stared. The woods grew silent again. He picked up the Kreighoff and wiped the dust from its barrel. "I didn't see that."

Gerry could only stare down the road. "What do you mean?"

"A bear just got away from me on a bicycle. That's impossible. Because it's impossible, I didn't see it."

"Buy yourself into believing that," Gerry said.

*   *   *

The old man was sitting on the porch, reading *Moby-Dick* when Gerry got home. He looked up as Gerry sat beside him. "Any luck hunting?" he asked.

"A little," Gerry said. He picked up the Winchester and ran its cleaning rod down its barrel.

"But you didn't bring anything home."

Gerry shrugged. He studied the barrel to keep from looking at the old man's eyes.

The old man read. Gerry cleaned the rifle and glanced every now and then out at the night. The only sounds were the steady beat of the crickets and the hiss of the kerosene lamp. It threw a warm circle of light. The stars were everywhere.

The old man finished his book and closed it. "By the way," he said, "there's a bear up in your bedroom."

Gerry glanced at him, then turned back to the Winchester. "Yeah?"

"She rode in on a bicycle about fifteen minutes ago, parked it by the steps, and went into the house. I had to scratch her belly first." His mustache stood out like a big, white glowworm; the creases in his face caught the shadows. "That isn't something you see every day."

Gerry nodded. "Not every."

"I think it's the same bear you had in there the other night—she walked in like she knew the place. An Asian sun bear, isn't it?"

"Yeah."

"From the circus?"

"Yeah."

The old man set his book beside the lantern. "I moved the bicycle around the back, just in case Jack Taylor drives by." He laughed. "God, what I wouldn't give to have seen the look on his face."

"It was something."

"I take it we have a pet bear now."

"Seems that way."

The old man nodded. He picked up his book and studied the cover. "This ended about how I expected it to. The whale wins." He flipped through the pages. "Every once in a while I like to read a story where the animal comes out on top."

Gerry sighted down the rifle barrel. "Me too," he said.

KEVIN MCCOLLEY is the author of four novels for young adults: *The Walls of Pedro García, Pecking Order, Sun Dance,* and *Switch.* His fifth young adult novel will be published in 1998, as will his first adult novel. Before becoming a full-time writer, McColley served in the navy for six years, and worked as a farmhand, a printer, a postal clerk, and a nuclear reactor operator, among other jobs. He lives in New Mexico.

"The story 'Hunting Bear' arose from a party game," he says. "We were sitting around trying to think of the strangest news story any of us had ever heard. A friend of mine had read an article about an American who had gone to hunt bear in Russia, and, after shooting at a bear and missing, watched it escape on a bicycle. I don't know if this is true or not, but as soon as I heard it, I knew I had a short story.

"My closest relationship to a gun," he says, "is that I was shot by one. I was hitchhiking in Denver a few years ago when I stumbled into a gang war and was shot in the leg by a boy carrying an Austrian machine gun. One bullet flicked by my nose, one tugged at the hem of my jeans, and a third buried itself in a tree a few inches from my head. The fourth bullet got me and fragmented; I still carry in my leg four pieces of shrapnel."

GOD'S PLAN FOR WOLFIE AND X-RAY

by David Rice

The movie *Repo Man* was their inspiration. Wolfie and Ray were particularly moved by the store robbery scene. Three kids go into a store armed with shotguns and take what cash there is. *"Fácil"* is what Ray said out loud. Wolfie nodded with a smile.

Each could see what the other was thinking, not because they had been friends since they were four, but because everyone in town could see. It was as if they had transparent skulls and all the folks of Edcouch could see their nerve impulses speeding through their neurons and jumping with a flash of light from one synaptic function to another. A string of disco lights tangled around their tiny gears that spun in the wrong direction.

Wolfie's cousin Renee called him X-Ray because she said people could see right through him, but she would tell Ray that the reason for the nickname was because Ray could see through people.

The idea of their robbing a store was *fácil* to them because in their bright minds they had experience in thievery. When they were seven years old they staked out the town cotton gin, and when it was dark enough not to be seen, but to see, they took an old army canvas tent, which Ray's father had stolen from the National Guard years before, and went down to the cotton gin and stuffed it full of cotton.

They did this several times until they had more than enough cotton to fill two cardboard refrigerator boxes that Wolfie's father got from the Sears store. Then they would take turns jumping into the boxes from their tree house. All was going well until Wolfie got his wiener dog, Bullet, and dropped him into the cotton-filled boxes, breaking two of his legs. Wolfie's mother gave them a lecture on the consequences of their actions.

"Look, because of what you two did, this poor dog is suffering. Everything any of us does has consequences. Wolfie, God only knows what I did to make you so *sonso!*"

She took them both to the cotton gin to return the cotton and so they could personally apologize to Mr. Fields, the cotton gin manager, but when they apologized, their eyes did not look remorseful.

When they were ten they broke into an abandoned warehouse that stored tin lids for quart-size tin cans.

They stole five cases of these lids, each case containing 250 lids. It took them the better part of the day before they figured out what the lids were best for: saucer fights.

They practiced throwing them at trees, but it became too easy to hit stationary targets. What they needed was moving targets, and the dogs and cats were never around to hit because they knew not to be anywhere near Wolfie and Ray. So they gathered some other kids, three from their neighborhood and five from the other side of Highway 107, and for two days practiced throwing until the lids became flying blades.

Ray's backyard became the battleground for the first saucer fight ever. The stinging pain of the flying saucers was no worse than that caused by being shot by a BB gun, so they were not afraid to rush each other, flinging saucers at blurring speeds. There were many direct hits, and after a few minutes of the battle it became a fact that even the best dodge player could not escape the deadly accuracy of Ray's flying saucers. Guillermo Guerrero became a permanent example of this truth.

• Guillermo Guerrero was known as Gilly by all the other kids, but after one of Ray's flying saucers hit him square in the forehead—causing him to run home screaming with blood gushing down his face, and then later to receive fifteen stitches across his forehead, which left a two-inch scar—his nickname was changed to Frankie, short for Frankenstein.

Ray's parents paid for the medical expenses and

made Ray and Wolfie return the lids, but not before making sure the lids were tin and not aluminum, because you could get up to fifteen cents per pound for aluminum.

When Wolfie's mother heard about the incident, she called the police. She was hoping the police could put the boys in jail for a few hours to give them a good scare. But the police said they couldn't do anything because the warehouse folks did not want to press charges and besides, "You know how kids are."

When Wolfie's mother realized that the police were not going to help, she prayed to St. Michael (the saint of vengeance) for advice. The good saint's punishment fit the crime. Wolfie, who was an altar boy at St. Theresa Catholic Church in Edcouch, was to serve fifteen masses in a row, one for every stitch Gilly had received, and was not allowed to call Gilly by the nickname Frankie.

When they were thirteen years old, Wolfie and Ray were both shot in the backside while stealing oranges from Mr. Gribbens's orchards, but it was only rock salt, and they were far enough away that it only felt like bee stings.

Wolfie's mother ran a tub of cool water and gently helped him in and took a small delight each time she poured onto his back a cup of water.

"Ay, it's stinging," Wolfie said in pain.

"*¿Ya, vez?* There are consequences for each of your actions," his mother said as she poured another cup.

Now at sixteen both were more mature, and after

viewing hundreds of robberies on television and being dedicated viewers of *America's Most Wanted* and *Cops,* they knew they had learned from the mistakes of others. Their holdup would be flawless.

It was three weeks away from Halloween, and this would give them a perfect excuse for a disguise. Both Wolfie and Ray owned twenty-gauge shotguns. Wolfie's father got his son a shotgun shortly after Ray's father bought Ray one for his fourteenth birthday. Wolfie's mother protested vehemently, but her husband said that owning a shotgun would teach him responsibility.

After many months of hunting rabbits and whatever else moved, they became good hunters and sure shots, something Ray's grandmother would attest to, with all the dead rabbits she had cooked for them.

Most of their spare time went into planning the store robbery. They scouted out the stores of the surrounding small towns where neither had relatives. Their evenings were spent walking into small stores, buying Cokes and candy bars and making mental maps of the store layouts. They checked for TV cameras and rented movies with robbery scenes.

Every day they played out the robbery in their heads. Knowing that sometimes robbers would accidentally call each other by their real names, Wolfie and Ray dubbed themselves Psycho and Killer so the store clerk would think twice about trying to take them on.

It was agreed that they would not use actual shells during the robbery. Neither was too keen on the idea of killing someone. They decided that the first two shells of their shotguns would be rock salt and the last one would be a live round, to be used only as a last resort, in which case they would aim for a leg or a foot, but not too close because they didn't want to blow someone's leg clear off.

After two weeks they picked the Vamos Y Vete store in the small town of Monte Alto because it was fifteen miles from Edcouch and eight miles from their hideout. The VV, as it was called by just about everyone, had no surveillance cameras, and the old man who worked at night seemed easy enough to take. Not to mention the VV had fishing equipment they wanted.

At their hideout (which was an abandoned Airstream International mobile home in the middle of the woods), they dressed themselves as sad clowns with green hair, and each wore black pants and a black long-sleeve shirt, trying to look as much alike as possible.

Wolfie shouted out, "You ready, Killer!"

Ray pumped the shotgun. *"¡Vamos y vete,* Psycho!"

"Remember, dude, be cool," Wolfie said.

"Puro, taking it easy," Ray replied.

Ray parked his father's truck two blocks away in a cornfield that was behind the VV, and they walked quietly toward the store as if they were hunting rabbits. Once they got close enough, they darted behind a propane gas tank and peered around the tank.

Wolfie gave his shotgun to Ray and trotted to the corner of the store, then crept along the wall to the edge of the shadow and store lights. He lay down and scooted under a broken-down Ford Bronco. He was equipped with a pen flashlight to signal Ray when to move in for the easy action.

After a couple of minutes Ray's body beaded in sweat that pushed the clown makeup out from his pores, streaking his sad clown face. His green wig began to itch his scalp and his leg was falling asleep and he could hear the mosquitoes calling to their friends, who were doing just fine with Wolfie.

Ray leaned the shotguns against the tank and darted to the corner of the store wall.

"Wolfie. Hey, Wolfie."

Wolfie looked over at Ray. "Psycho, Psycho!"

"Yeah, yeah. *Oye, vato,* what are you waiting for? I haven't seen any cars drive up."

"Wait for the signal, dude. You know, man, be cool man or you're going to mess it up. Now, get back to the tank and wait for the signal, *vato.*"

"Well, hurry it up," Ray said.

Ray went back to the tank, and Wolfie knew he had to go with his gut instinct when to make the move, but at the moment his instinct was telling him to forget the whole idea. He looked across the empty parking lot and pointed the pen flashlight toward Ray to signal now or never.

Ray saw the dim light flash, grabbed Wolfie's shotgun and his, and sprinted through the shadow to Wolfie. The only sound was the faint barking of dogs throughout the neighborhood and the buzzing of the

fluorescent lights. Ray and Wolfie knew this was it
because blood filled their chests and the barrels of their
shotguns were no longer cool to their clammy hands.

"*Bueno, ale!*" Wolfie said with a raised voice. The
shotguns at their sides, they quickly walked by the
store windows. Wolfie glanced inside but did not see
any heads over the five-foot shelves. It was his last
chance to listen to his only good inner voice.

Ray swung open the store door and rushed in with
Wolfie right behind.

"Okay, old man," Ray yelled, "freeze right there!
Don't even get up. Just be cool, man!"

Señor Vásquez, sitting in his blue lawn chair, was
startled by the shouts. He dropped the plate of birthday cake his wife had made the night before.

"*¿Qué?* What do you two boys think you're doing?
And why are you dressed like clowns?" he asked.

"Because it's Halloween, old man! Now you just sit
there and shut up!" Ray said with a shove of his shotgun.

"Boys, you don't want to rob this store. There's
only forty or fifty dollars in the cash register. Unless
you want some fishing equipment."

"Shut up, old man," Ray shouted. "We don't need
no stinking fishing equipment! Just what you got in
the register."

"Okay, okay. Take the money." Señor Vásquez mo-
tioned to the cash register. "But I'm telling you there's
nothing in there. Why don't you just take some fishing
poles or some caps."

"I said shut up! Man, what are you, deaf? Psycho, you get the money and I'll keep an eye on the old man."

Wolfie moved around the counter and made Señor Vásquez get up and move out. Ray kept his shotgun on the old man, who moved slowly while saying, "Okay, okay, take it easy, take it easy."

Wolfie pressed some buttons, but the register let out a continuous beep. Wolfie continued hitting keys, but the high-pitched sound would not cease.

"Hit the No Sale button," Señor Vásquez said.

"What?" Wolfie replied.

"He said to hit the No Sale button," Ray answered.

Wolfie looked at the many keys but couldn't focus on the letters very well since he wasn't wearing his glasses.

"Wolfie, hurry up and hit the No Sale button. We don't have—"

"It's Psycho, *vato!* Psycho! What's wrong with you?"

"Crap! Hey, old man. You didn't hear nothing!"

"What?" Señor Vásquez said.

"Okay, old man, move!" Ray said. "Go help Psycho open the register, and don't try anything, man, or I'll blow your head off!"

Señor Vásquez shook his head and moved toward the cash register, taking it slow because that's how he did everything. Wolfie stood aside and kept his shotgun aimed at the old man.

Señor Vásquez pressed two keys, and the cash drawer sprang with a ring. *"Ay te va,"* he said.

"Okay, old man. Move away from the register and keep your hands up," Ray said.

Wolfie laid his shotgun on the counter, grabbed a paper bag, and began taking the money. His hands were sweaty, and his fingers became stiff, making it difficult to grip the bills. It was supposed to be quick, in and out and nobody gets hurt, but he was certain an hour had passed since they'd entered the store.

Ray saw the movement from the corner of his eye. Four people walking past the windows.

"Crap! Wolfie, be cool. Old man, act normal and you better be cool." Ray ran and hid behind the candy display. Wolfie tried to get down, but it was too late. One had made eye contact with him.

Entering the store were four people in costume: the Lone Ranger, Tonto, Batman, and Batgirl. Batman held the door for the others as they walked in talking and laughing.

Ray could see them through a convex mirror in the corner of the store. When all four were in, Ray jumped up yelling. "Okay, everybody on the floor! Let's go! On the floor. Move!" He shouted so hard that his voice squeaked.

The Lone Ranger let out a short shout and proceeded to dive to the floor, followed by Tonto and Batgirl.

"Move! Let's go! On the floor, everybody," Ray shouted again.

Batman turned and ran for the door. Ray shouted for him to freeze, but Batman's cape was unfurled and

in full swing. Ray yelled again, but Batman was halfway out the door. Ray pulled up his shotgun and fired
at Batman. The sound caused Wolfie to jerk and the
old man to yell out, *"¡Ay Dios!"*

Batman screamed and arched his back, but didn't
stop. He ran past the window in a black blur.

"Crap!" Ray yelled. "Wolf—Psycho, quick, get the
money and let's get the hell out of here."

Batgirl had a feeling she knew the clown's voice,
and now she was *certain* who the robbers were: Wolfie,
her first cousin, and his stupid friend Ray. With her
cape covering her arms, she reached for her bat belt,
where she had her cellular phone attached, and began
dialing her aunt's phone number. She brought the
phone up to her side and muffled the ringing, then
looked up at Wolfie, who looked right back at her.

"I know it's you, Wolfie, and this is your stupid
friend, X-Ray."

Ray pointed the shotgun at her. "Shut up!"

She heard a faint hello coming from the phone and
knew it was her aunt. She moved the phone away from
her side and closer up so her aunt could hear.

"Wolfie, your mother is going to be real mad when
she finds out what you are doing," Renee said. "You
just wait. You two are going to get in real trouble for
this. Robbing a store. How stupid can you be?"

Renee could hear Wolfie's mother calling for her
husband, telling him to get on the cordless phone so
they could both listen.

"I said shut up!" Ray yelled. "Psycho, come on, let's go!"

"I wouldn't go out there if I was you, Wolfie. The guy X-Ray shot was Jesús Jiménez, and he's a gun nut. He's probably got a bazooka set up so he can blow up your green hair. And why are you guys dressed up like clowns? I mean, what's up with that?"

"Shut up, Renee. Man, *esta* baby can never shut up!" Ray said.

"Vez, I knew it was you, Ray!"

Renee heard her aunt's voice. She was cursing her husband, saying, "You and those damn guns. See what your actions have caused!"

"Would you shut up," she heard her uncle respond. "We have to find out where they are so we can call the police."

Wolfie came around the corner of the counter, making the old man move along as he did. He looked at his cousin and then at Ray.

"Come on, let's go," Ray said.

"Wolfie, wait," Renee said. "Before you leave, you want to tell your mother why you robbed the VV?" She slid the cellular phone across the floor to his feet. "She's been listening this entire time."

Wolfie looked at the steady red light of the cellular phone and lowered his arms. Ray walked over and stomped on the phone, smashing the flat box. He grabbed Wolfie by the arm and pulled him toward the glass door.

"That's it! *¡Vámonos!* Time to get the hell out of here!" Ray said.

"Ray, you're going to pay for that phone," Renee shouted.

Ray and Wolfie stepped outside, and there was Batman behind the old Ford Bronco. "All right, freeze! Just hold it right there!" He was pointing a gun at them.

Ray pointed his shotgun at Batman. "Drop it!"

"You drop it! Look, there's nowhere to go. I called the police already, and they're on their way, so just forget it."

Ray took a tight grip of his shotgun. "Drop the damn gun or I swear I'll fire!"

Batman took a tight grip of *his* gun, though he was shaking too much to get an accurate aim. "I'm not dropping it. *You* drop it. And besides, Our Lord Jesus Christ will not fail me, and I know all you got in there is rock salt."

"What? Listen, *vato,* the rest of the shells are real, and I'll use 'em if you don't drop it," Ray shouted.

Wolfie aimed his shotgun, but it was too dark to see anything. Ray fired, and Batman took cover behind the Bronco as the rock salt scattered across the metal. Batman fired back wildly, shattering the store window. Wolfie screamed and Ray fired again, this time blasting the Bronco window. Batman pulled his gun around the fender and fired aimlessly at Wolfie and Ray.

Ray was not as fortunate as Wolfie. One wild lucky bullet cut through Ray's right shoulder, splitting his shoulder blade into three pieces. He'd be left with a surgery scar and sharp pains every time he tried to do pushups while killing time in the state penitentiary.

Wolfie fell to the cement when the other stray bullet went through the inside of his left leg, missing his femur and artery by an inch. It was a pain he didn't feel until he heard Ray whimpering and moaning about his own wound.

A highway patrol car arrived two minutes later. A cop brought out a first-aid kit to help slow the bleeding from the two crying boys. Wolfie's parents came before the ambulance did, and Wolfie's mother held her sobbing son gently in her arms as one of the ambulance crew bandaged his leg.

Wolfie's father stood next to the medic with Renee and Batman behind him, and asked if his son was going to be okay.

"Hey, he's real lucky compared to that other clown," the medic replied. "If Batman here was a better shot, these two might be dead."

Batman stepped forward. "Sir, I didn't mean to hurt your son. I'm really sorry. I didn't want to hurt anybody. I was just doing the Lord's work."

Wolfie's mother looked up at Batman. "What?"

Renee put her hand on Batman's shoulder and edged forward. *"Sí tía.* This is my friend Jesús. He's a criminal justice major at the university, and he's also studying to be a deacon."

Jesús nodded. "Yes. It's true. And ma'am and sir, I'm really sorry about shooting your son, but maybe it's all for the best. I mean, none of us know God's plan, and this could have been a good thing to happen to your son and his friend."

Wolfie's mother held her son and knew she agreed with Jesús.

And indeed good things did happen in the years to follow. Jesús finished college and became a deacon at St. Theresa and married Renee. He also helped baptize Wolfie's son, and he became Ray's probation officer each time he was released from jail until finally Jesús converted Ray into a born-again Christian. These events only reinforced Jesús' belief that God had a plan for everyone, including Wolfie and Ray.

DAVID RICE was born and raised in Texas and now lives in Austin. He is the author of *Give the Pig a Chance & Other Stories,* a collection inspired by his Mexican American culture and by his childhood home, the Rio Grande Valley.

"When I was twelve years old," he says, "I was awakened one morning by a dove outside my bedroom window. It just wouldn't stop singing, and I wanted to go back to sleep. After a few minutes, I got up, grabbed my faithful BB gun, walked to the back door, and took steady aim. I shot. Easy. The dove dropped like a rock.

"Going back to my bedroom, I heard my grandfather call out to me. I opened his door but made sure
he didn't see my BB gun. He lit his pipe and then
asked what I had just done.

"I wanted to lie, but it was too difficult. 'Well,
I . . . I was asleep and then this stupid bird
started making all this racket. So I took my BB gun
and shot it.'

"My grandfather was an emotional man. His eyes
began to fill. 'David, do you know what that dove was
doing? It was singing a beautiful song that no other
animal can sing. A song that me or you could never.
sing. A song that God taught it to sing. And you went
and killed it.'

"I tried to say something, but couldn't find the
words. He told me to close his door, and I did. I
leaned against the wall and stared at my BB gun, then
put it in my room and went outside.

"I looked at the dove, then picked it up and held its
still-warm body. I got a shovel and dug a small hole
and placed the bird in it. I took two twigs from the
tree the bird has been singing in and made a cross to
put at the head of the grave. I cried for a bit and told
God I was sorry, and promised that I would never
again kill any living animal for as long as I lived.

"The incident didn't make me get rid of my BB
gun, but all I shot from then on were bottles, cans,
and, once, my foot."

WAR GAME

by Nancy Werlin

What I did to Lije. It might have seemed . . . okay, in some ways it *was* cruel; I'll give you that. But I had to do it. It was important. Okay?

You don't see? Fine. I'll explain.

Lije—Elijah Schooler—and I were friends, though nobody knew it except him and me. It had just kind of worked out that way over the years, with Lije being a boy and two years younger and going to the private school his father paid for. His bedroom window faced mine over three feet of alley, and he used to sleep with the light on. Sometimes at night we'd talk for hours— or rather I would—when Lije was worried and had trouble sleeping. For years we did that. And he lent me books. His school had an incredible library, and he could get me anything I wanted.

It wasn't a big secret, our friendship. It was a little secret, something pleasant, but not really important. Until last August when I was fourteen.

It'd been an almost unbearably hot summer. At first
it was just the little kids who had the guns—you
know, the big plastic machine guns with huge tanks
for water. Super-Soakers. Water Uzis. Ricky Leone and
Curt Quillian and even Curt's little sister, Janey, were
jumping out from alleys and from around corners and
behind cars, screaming like police sirens and soaking
everybody in sight. The rest of us had to defend ourselves. Before you knew it, nearly every kid in the
neighborhood between six and fourteen had a water
gun. They were under fifteen dollars at the supermar-
ket.

They were just plain fun, the guns. I'd had no idea.
Though I'd seen real guns before, around the neighborhood and at school and stuff, I'd actually never had
a toy gun before, even when I was little. But I felt so
powerful, cradling the gun under my arm and pumping away. Every time you hit someone, they'd yowl.
Run. Unless they were armed too; then they'd whip
around and shoot back. It was incredible. I'm not a
violent person—none of us were, really (except maybe
Lina at times). We weren't gang kids; in fact, we did
our best to keep away from the gangs. It was the city.
It was summer. It was hot. That's all.

At first, we big kids just did like the little kids and
ambushed each other. But then I said something, and
we got more ambitious. Kevin DiFranco and Lina Os-
wego organized two teams—armies—and we were all
assigned ranks. The little kids were privates and scouts,
and the older kids were lieutenants or spies. I was a

lieutenant colonel and head of the war council.
"You're smart, Jo," Kevin said. "You do the strategy."
Of course Kevin and Lina made themselves generals.
Within a week, there were nearly thirty of us involved.

At first I just did it for something to do. And maybe
also because it felt good to get the attention from
Kevin. He'd never had much to do with me before. I
wasn't interested in him, you understand; I wasn't interested in any real boys right then. That was the summer I had the tremendous crush on Talleyrand, and in
all my fantasies I (or rather, my alter ego, Anne
Fourier) was deeply involved in the politics of the
French Revolution. Anne generally disguised herself as
Pierre-Ange Gaultier, a boy journalist and the best of
Talleyrand's spies. I had worked out nine separate and
extremely elaborate scenarios, all of them leading to
the danger- and passion-filled moment in which Talleyrand would realize he was in love with Anne. But
where were Anne's loyalties? With him or with the
Revolution or with only herself? It depended on how I
was feeling that day. Usually in the end I was on my
own side, though, because in a war that's how you
survive. That's how Talleyrand did it.

Kevin DiFranco was both popular and cute, but he
couldn't have competed with my fantasy world if he'd
tried.

But my imaginary life was private—I wouldn't even
have told Lije the details, and he borrowed most of my
books for me. A massive crush on a centuries-dead
Machiavellian priest-politician in a powdered wig

wasn't the kind of thing you shared. And if I'd gone on to tell people about my mental war games, my elaborately researched historical alter ego, well, my facade of social respectability would have cracked right there, and I'd have been the butt of a million idiotic jokes. If you want to survive, you have to blend in.

Plus, even I couldn't live in the eighteenth century all the time. And our real-life war game fascinated me. I had a lot of say in it, a lot of control. I was the one who said we were the opposing guerrilla factions of a country in the throes of civil war, a country located right on the equator, full of steaming jungles (the playground and the abandoned factory lot around the corner on Eastern Avenue). The jungles, I said, entirely surrounded the bombed-out capital city (our street and its alleys). I was the one who set up the POW camp behind the brick wall in the truck yard, and I wrote up the rules surrounding capture, punishment, and death. Kevin and Lina were the generals, okay, and they planned the raids and battles and took care of the daily details. But I was the one who designed the game. You could even say it was *my* game.

It was amazing, when you thought about it, when you saw how well it worked. I mean, it had never happened before—all the kids in the neighborhood hanging out and doing something together. We were all different ages, of course, and on top of that there were cliques. But it worked. For a few weeks, it worked. And we had such fun.

Only Lije wasn't playing. He didn't have the sum-

mer off from school; he was in some special en-
richment program and came trotting home every
afternoon at around three o'clock and let himself into
his apartment with his key. He'd be there alone until
after eight o'clock, because his mother worked as a
secretary for some big downtown law firm, and she
didn't get home until late. And of course his father
was, as the social workers say, not in the picture. Actually, Lije had never met him. But he did pay the tu-
ition for Lije's private school, and, hey, I've heard of
worse absentee-father deals. Mine, for instance. Lije
hated it, though. Hated *him*. It was a funny thing. Lije
was a fat, scared mess with a runny nose, and he
couldn't sleep without the light on. But underneath
that he was okay. Because he could hate.

We were on the second day of a two-day truce
(really an excuse to concentrate on covert ops and
training) on the afternoon we all noticed Lije. He had
just come out of the convenience store on the corner
of Eastern Avenue and Tenth Street. He looked dorky,
especially considering the heat, in his long pants and
cheap dress shirt and school tie and with his backpack
dragging his shoulders down. He was holding a
wrapped ice-cream sandwich that he'd obviously just
bought, and he was completely absorbed in trying to
pick open the wrapping.

He was a perfect target, and Lina pounced. "Am-
bush!" she yelled, and in seconds her SWAT team had
him surrounded. Lije looked up, blinking, at the four
Super-Soakers leveled at his head.

"Hand over the ice cream," Lina said, "or you're dead."

Lije shot a glance at me, where I was lounging on a stoop with Kevin and a couple of the little kids. But then his eyes skimmed on past. Right then it hit me that we had never talked to each other in public, only from our windows across the alley. Out here on the street, that relationship was nonexistent. It didn't even need saying. So I grinned at Lije but didn't move or speak.

Silently, he handed over the ice cream to Lina. She laughed, made a gesture, and the SWAT team opened fire. Lije didn't move. He stood there and took it, until the tanks were empty and he was completely soaked.

We all laughed. "Feels good, huh?" Lina said. If you knew her, you'd know she was actually being friendly. For Lina.

And that was the moment I understood that Lije wasn't okay after all; that he would need help to be okay. Because he wouldn't just laugh too. Couldn't even force himself to do it; couldn't even pretend. Instead, he acted like a jerk; minded; showed he minded. Why didn't he know better than to show it? Why did he have to let his lip tremble and his face get red? Why did he run like that? Why did he let them—let us—let me—see he was scared?

It's dangerous to show your fear. It marks you as a victim. And watching Lije run away like a little kid, I was afraid for him. And right then I knew I had to do something to help him. I just didn't know what, or when.

That night, though, was completely ordinary. Lije's light came on well before the sun set, and I leaned out of my window and called his name.

"You all right?" I said.

"Yeah." His hair was wet; he'd obviously just taken a shower. Another shower.

"Sorry about today," I said casually. "You just have to laugh, you know. You can't let it get to you." I watched him carefully to see if he understood what I was saying.

Lije shrugged. "Jerks," he said. He said it like he meant it, but I saw his chin tremble and his eyes brim. So he didn't get it. I decided to leave it for now.

"Did that book I wanted come in from interlibrary loan?"

He nodded and handed over a hardback copy of J. F. Bernard's biography of Talleyrand. Inches thick, crammed full of detail, and with plates not only of the man himself, but also of his wife and some of his more famous mistresses. I was thrilled. "Thanks tons," I said to Lije. "This is great. How long can I keep it?"

"Two weeks." Now that we were back on familiar ground, he was feeling more comfortable. He leaned on the windowsill. "Jo, listen. I think the librarian is getting suspicious. She asked me if I had finished the books I already had out."

"What'd you say?"

"Oh, I just shrugged and said I was working on it.

But then she started asking me what I found so interesting about France, and was I taking French, and stuff
like that, so I had to get out of there fast. You know,
I'm not supposed to take out books for other people."

This wasn't news to me. Why was he suddenly
making such a big deal out of it? "Look," I said, "I'd
get them myself if the public library still did interlibrary loan."

"I know. I just want to be careful and not get into
any trouble."

"Don't worry about it," I said. "They won't know
anything you don't tell them. It's in your control.
You're in charge."

"You always say that," Lije said, which was true.
But I'd always thought before that he heard me. I
looked at him and saw that he had that rabbity look
that he got when he was tense, brooding about his
father, or about his mother and money, or something.
Life was rougher for Lije than it should have been, just
because he took everything so hard, so seriously. He
didn't know how to protect himself at all. I wondered
how I'd missed that before.

So I said, "Okay. I'll tell you some stuff you can
dazzle the librarian with." And even though I wanted
nothing more than to be alone with the new book,
instead I climbed up onto the sill and leaned against
the window frame, while Lije pulled up a chair to his
window and propped his chin on his hands. I told him
about the bread riots and how they guillotined the rich
bastards and how, for the greater good, Charlotte Cor-

day—what a woman, huh?—stabbed Marat to death
in his bath. And as I talked, softly as I always did when
I told Lije stories, the sun set, and if it hadn't been for
the smog and the city lights, there might have been
stars.

"You tired enough to sleep now, Lije?" I asked finally, long after midnight. It never got quiet in our
neighborhood, not exactly, but most people were
sleeping.

He didn't answer, and for a moment I thought he
was already asleep. Then he said, "Jo?"

"Yeah?"

"You like me, Jo, don't you? You're my friend?"

He'd never asked me anything like that before. I
said, "Is this about today?" Lije didn't answer, but he
did look at me, his cheeks all pudgy and his eyes, well
. . . suspicious. I said, "I already told you I was sorry
that happened. But Lije, you took it too seriously, you
know what I mean?" But he was still staring at me
with that odd look on his face, *needing,* and so finally I
said, "Yeah. Yes, Lije. I like you. I am your friend. I've
always been your friend." Which was the truth.

"Good," Lije said. "I'm your friend too, Jo. Always."

And then he stood up and leaned out the window
and reached his hand across the alley. He held out his
arm, suspended, for a few moments before I realized
he wanted me to take it and shake hands. I did that. I
think . . . now I think it may have been the only
time we ever touched.

Then he went to bed, and I read about Talleyrand until dawn, when my mother came home from her night shift and made me get some sleep.

The next day it was nearly noon by the time I finally got outside, and Kevin was pissed at me for missing morning council. Worse, our planned morning kidnapping of Lina's best sniper, Ricky Leone, hadn't worked; instead Ricky had shot two of our guys, and by our rules—my rules—they were dead for the rest of the day. An hour later Janey got caught spying and ended up in the POW camp. Lina was triumphant, Kevin furious. There were about fifteen of us engaged in a huge argument about the rules, with me trying to cool them off and Lina nearly purple with rage.

And that was when Lije came down the street again, looking dorkier than ever. I saw him see us standing there, armed of course; saw his eyes dart around as if looking for a hole to dive into. But then—because he really did have something underneath, like I said before—he squared his shoulders and came on anyway, marching like a windup toy soldier, looking neither left nor right. Hostility, fear, anger—they were almost visible, pulsing in the air around him as he tried to push his way right through us.

Kevin stuck out his foot and tripped him. Lije fell onto his hands and knees. A few of the littler kids snickered. Lina laughed, and it wasn't the friendly (for Lina) laugh of yesterday. She'd picked up on Lije's hostility, of course, and taken it as disrespect. "You looking for trouble?" she said to Lije's back. Two of her kids stepped forward and leveled their guns at Lije, grinning. "Soak him?" one said.

It was addressed to Lina, but Kevin answered: "Go ahead." Kevin hadn't even finished talking when Lina's kids opened fire on Lije.

First just those two. But then more of them, in a circle around Lije, shooting down first at Lije's back. Then somebody—Lina?—kicked Lije viciously, forcing him over. And the rest of the water reservoirs pummeled down on his face and chest. He was pinned to the concrete by the force of the water.

Talleyrand—master strategist and supreme survivor—always knew how to improvise on the moment. He would have been proud of me, because I knew immediately that this was the moment to help Lije. I didn't even have to think how to do it. I knew.

I waited until everyone else was done. Waited until Lije got up, slowly. His palms were scraped and bleeding. He didn't say anything. He looked at me. And it was that look, the one I'd seen on his face last night. *Help me,* it said. *Protect me. Be my friend. I can't do it alone.* But he didn't say anything, he just watched me. Waited.

I emptied my own gun into his face. Then I said, "Run on home, kid. You don't belong out here. You might get hurt."

After a few more excruciating seconds, Lije left, dripping.

That night, I lay alone in bed watching the light in Lije's window and reliving those minutes. I waited until after it was full dark. Then I went to the open window and called his name. I didn't really think he would come, but he did. He looked terrible.

"Give me back my books," he said. It was what I was expecting. It still hurt, though. Inside, I felt the way he looked. But I didn't show it. I handed him the Talleyrand biography—at least I'd had one night with it—and the others he'd got me before. I wondered how I'd get books now. Somehow. I'd figure something out.

"You're going to be okay, Lije," I said evenly.

Lije shook his head. He was standing awkwardly, arms tense, hands dangling out of sight below the windowsill. "You lied to me," he said.

I shrugged. Stared right back at him as his arms bent and lifted. I saw with pride that he had his own Super-Soaker now. He aimed it at me. His aim was lousy because he was crying, shaking, and so most of the water missed me, but I stood there and took it, as he had, until his reservoir was as empty as mine.

"I hate you, Jo," Lije said. "You're not my friend."

He went back into his room. I went and got a towel and dried myself. Then I waited. And after a while Lije put his light out and, to show me that he could, for the first time slept—if he did sleep that night—in the dark.

Okay, *yes,* I was sorry to hurt him. But the French have a saying about things like this. *C'est la guerre.* Literally it means "that's war," but really it means "that's life." And . . . Lije doesn't understand. Not now. But *you* can. He was wrong about my not being his friend.

I am the best friend he will ever have.

NANCY WERLIN grew up in Peabody, Massachusetts, earned a B.A. from Yale University, and now works as a "webmaster" and writer for a Boston software company. Her first novel for teenagers, *Are You Alone on Purpose?*, was a *Publishers Weekly* Flying Start book and an ALA Quick Pick.

About "War Game," she says, "I'll confess the awful truth: I have never seen—let alone touched—a real gun in my life. At first I tried to fake it. That was story number one, which died a death too horrible to relate. So there I was, with one weekend between me and the deadline, and no story. I realized then that my last hope was to write a piece centered around the only kind of gun I'd ever handled myself.

"Originally, I thought this story was about peer pressure. But within a few paragraphs of beginning to write, I understood that the narrator, Jo (who had come along from story number one), was not really interested in fitting in with the group—though she knows the pretense is important. Something else was on Jo's mind; something more important to her personally. So a second story developed, one that pivoted on Jo's view of the world and of friendship. Writing 'War Game' left me with a question that I find intensely disturbing: What if Jo is right about the world?"

CUSTODY

by Frederick Busch

Here it is. He's sitting on the hill across the road from their house. His butt's cold from the rocky ground. He feels like he's floating between the grass he can't see and the stars that he can see. Every minute, more fog blows off and more stars roll in above him. He feels like his head is huge; it's this enormous icy balloon that's floating in the black air. Pop's gun is black too. It's colder than the ground. It's freezing, and it fills his face. The barrel is short, but it fills his mouth up. He looks at their new, creaky farmhouse with its dark windows, and he gags on the gun that's stuffing his tongue up into his head. He closes his eyes. Then he opens them. He doesn't want to miss anything, he decides. So he sits with his numb butt and with the taste of metal and oil and with the weight of the old revolver on his hand and his lower lip. He looks straight ahead at the dark house.

He's trying to guess what he'll see. He fired pistols

with Pop on the range in New York City. They wore goggles and he still saw yellow spots. He saw a kid shoot a homemade piece called a zip gun outside high school. Everything went bright yellow. The gun blew up. It took away parts of two of the kid's fingers, and it broke his wrist. So here it is, he figures. He's going to see bright yellow and then nothing. He figures the recoil might bust his front teeth. He *knows* it'll bust up his mouth.

He takes the gun out of his mouth, and he wipes his lips. "Bust up the back of my *head* for shootin' sure," he says. He hears himself: *shootin' sure.* "Jerk," he whispers.

His ankles hurt from being crossed. His arm hurts from holding the .38 in his mouth. His mouth hurts where the gun's weight pressed on his lower lip.

He says, in Pop's voice, "Let's not hear the slackers and complainers, now."

He puts the gun in his mouth. He instructs his eyes to stay open so he gets to see as much as he can. But the air on his eyes makes them water, and the tears remind him of his mom's blinking tears away and telling them she wasn't crying while she cried. He remembers Miz Bean crying. She didn't talk about it. She held it in and then she couldn't, and tears leaked straight down her face.

He takes the pistol away from his face, and he says, "But anyway, I'm not crying."

It's what he told them at the hearing. His mom had two lawyers, and Pop had this terrible man with blue-

white hair and a face so red Pete thought the guy
would explode. It was a special meeting with a psychologist, and everybody's lawyer was yapping and
snarling about custody and the needs of the child.
That was his job all that morning, to be the child
while they fought with each other. Pete was going to
sit next to Pop, but his mom pulled a chair away from
next to her and she smiled. That was all it took. She
smiled, and he went over into the smell of her perfume
and maybe vodka and her hands all over his face, and
he was hugged. The white-haired lawyer, Leary,
clapped his hands, and everybody turned around.

"Over here, young Pete," the lawyer said. He wasn't
smiling, but he was trying to, and his face looked like
it was beating. It was like a heart in a movie about
operations. Leary's face was red and beating, and he
was furious.

Pete's mom said, "Stay with me, darling, couldn't
you?"

Pop said, "Oh, shit," but not with angry tones, and
then the psychologist came in. She was little and
chunky with a strong-looking neck and a friendly face.

She said to Pete, "You doing okay?"

Pete knew he was going to blubber. "I'm not crying," he told her.

So here it is. He's on the hillside, across from the
house Pop drove them to one night. Pop woke him up
and partway pushed and partway pulled him into the
station wagon that was packed, he found out, with his

clothes and books and with some of Pop's. They drove for hours in the darkness from Mill Basin in Brooklyn into upstate New York, and he slept, shivering, but not from cold. His mom left the country, Pop said. She ran off with a man she didn't want to fall in love with but did. She couldn't help it, Pop told him. Pete wanted to ask why they were running away in the dark if she was the one who ran away. He didn't. He knew he didn't dare. His mom's phone doesn't answer at the number she gave him, and he figures Pop would tell him the truth, even if what he told him didn't sound truthful.

You can question his father, and you can even argue with him for a while if you're polite. He wouldn't slam you around. He might lift you up in the air a little and shake you. He might lean down into your face so you were nose and nose, and he might growl a little. He's a New York cop who says he's retired now. But he was a New York cop. He had these long arms and wide hands, and his fingers were flat at the ends. He used to play the flute when they were happy, and his mom went around kissing the top of his father's head while he played. He hadn't played for years. The music was pretty stupid. It was curly and it squeaked. But he wouldn't mind hearing his father play it sometime again. He doesn't think he will. They were going to get divorced, and they were going to fight over him until the divorce was done. It is Pete's suspicion that his father ran from the fight. He considers asking his father if he's kidnapped his own son. He knows he won't ask. He *would* ask his mother, but her phone only rings and rings.

In the central school, someone's father got mad at a teacher. Pete was in the class across the hall. The other kid's father walked in wearing these high, green rubber boots that smelled of cow flop. He just walked into the class and started shouting. Pete's English teacher called the office on the intercom. The farmer was shouting, and the teacher was shouting back. The farmer got louder. The teacher shut up. Pete's teacher made them sit there in the gluey smell of floor polish and steam heat. Pete saw his pop walk with these long slow steps from the hallway into the room across the hall. The noise stopped. Pete heard Pop's voice rumbling. The other father made a sharp, angry sound, and then he said something like *"Oh."* He said it again, and he came out into the hall behind Pete's father, who seemed to be dragging all of this big, smelly farmer by the littlest finger of his right hand. He kept saying *"Ow!"* and Pop kept hauling him away. He never had to ask people more than twice. A kid next to Pete in the English class said, "Cool."

So Pete is sitting on the hillside in the dark. He's deciding what to do. And what he *can't* figure out is why his mother would throw him away like that. New guy or not, vodka or not, they were pretty much best friends. He thinks about the time he got chased by some kids from Avenue U. He was wearing these bright green corduroys that one of them said looked faggy. He remembered how back then he didn't know what *faggy* meant. He told the kid that *he* was faggy. The kid's eyes got big and round, and he and these two other guys came after Pete, and Pete took off. He came around the corner, and it was like he sent a radio signal or something. There was his mother in her jeans and his father's big flannel shirt with the sleeves rolled up. She had her arms crossed, and she was blowing a bubble-gum bubble. When it popped and she got it back in her mouth, she said, "Don't you touch my kid."

Something happened, he figures, and he missed it. From "Don't you touch my kid" to this noplace place. And his mother is noplace in the world that he knows about, and he and Pop are living someplace that is not only not Brooklyn, New York, it's like the middle of some country nobody heard of except the people who have to live there; it's like what you see while the guy in the movies on the public broadcasting station talks about places that are mostly rock and grass and turtles. It's the deal they deal you in divorces. One of them takes off, one of them keeps you, and your house is in the middle of stones and trees and all of those stars and whatever is moving around in the bushes.

In the morning, before they left the house, he was thinking that his pop's aftershave smelled like the fags in the subway. Now he knew what *faggy* meant. He thought of telling the school psychologist, Miz Bean, about the subways. She would know about them because she got around and because Pop would have told her. She and Pop were dating, if you could use that word for older people like his father. But she wouldn't know how they smelled in the rush hour when the creeps were there wearing smelly aftershave and letting their hands fall on your butt and your balls like an accident. Up here, you smelled horses and cows and the diesel off the tractors you got stuck behind on the way to the completely noplace town where you shopped.

When they drove into school this morning, Pete looked ahead into the dust of their road. They went past the shitshacks. People up on their road lived in trailers with tents pitched next door because they had so many kids and no money. They built little log-cabin shitboxes onto the trailers and one of them kept a tin roof on with old tires because of the wind. Pop bought the white house and the land and the pond, and they lived with all these trailers and shitboxes just out of sight. It was embarrassing to have a house that big around here. Down in town after they had gotten onto the paved part of the road, they passed where a guy sold purple hearts and bombers and LSD lollipops and of course what he told the cornheads was excellent grass. Pete was pretty sure it was mostly straw with a little grass plus maybe oregano and cow piss mixed in or something.

Pop said, "I know about it."

"Huh?"

"I already know about it. The green house with the barn next door. I don't bust guys anymore."

"What, Pop?"

"Anyway, you don't touch that stuff, do you? It's the only reason I'd do those characters now. If they were helping you put something into your body that could hurt you."

Pete nodded. He didn't look at Pop.

The parking lot was huge, and the central school was huge. About fifteen school buses were dumping all kinds of farmers and bimbolinas and small smelly people into school. Pete thanked his father and waved because that was how Pop wanted them saying goodbye. His father waved back, and everybody who was left in their family smiled and showed their manners. Pete walked into the middle of the cornheads and disappeared, it felt like, from his father's sight.

Later on, he saw Miz Bean talking to Pop near the cafeteria. She was tall, but Pop was taller. But she was tall, and she had big shoulders. She had a long, thin nose that made her look like a queen of France or someplace in Europe. She wasn't like a model on TV, which Pop made him turn off a lot because turning off the TV was going to make him get all As and become prime college material at thirteen; Pop had this problem with college. Miz Bean was smiling a lot with Pop.

Stish, whose father owned a bar that looked like an accident nobody ever cleaned up, aimed his chin at Miz Bean.

He said to Pete, "What's she like, man?"

"Who?"

Stish's face turned into some android clown. He

rolled his eyes back and let his tongue flop onto his cheek. "Excuse me," he said. "I thought there was a human female over there with your father. Is that your father over there with the human female? Yeah? Then the human female I would be referring to is the one your fucking father is trying not to feel up during the passing bell. You know which group of creatures my scanner is indicating now?"

Pete said, "Tell me he's my fucking father one more time."

"Chill out, all right? We all know *he's* a tough-ass from the city. But don't—"

Pete heard his voice get low like Pop's. "Tell me what do, Stish. Call me a name and call my father a name and then tell me what to do."

Stish put his hands in the air. "Oh, take me into custody, Occifer." His eyes were wide now, and he made himself look scared. But Pete knew he was, just a little.

"Who'd want you," Pete said. He turned his back on Stish and went to class.

Pop went back to talking to Miz Bean while his head kept moving. He saw what happened up and down the hall. He was the guidance person in charge of attendance and guys who came in late and the sneak smokers and whoever carried weapons in for fighting. Miz Bean stayed there too. She was the head guidance counselor. She was the one you had to talk to about your life and, say, your mother, those kind of items.

In history, they did Clay. He was the Great Compromiser, Miz Carver told them. She had all kinds of body on her. They changed at the bell and spent the next two class modules with Mr. Arthur. He told them what they needed to know about getting diseases from sex. HIV was pretty serious stuff, and Pete made himself listen. He didn't want to. He wanted to think. If Pop was with Miz Bean, who was Mom with? He wondered if maybe Pop was wrong and she was alone. He wondered if she was lonely or frightened or anything. If she was, he thought, how come she didn't call him up? Shouldn't mothers do that?

On his way to lunch, he passed Miz Bean's office. She had long feet and long legs, and they were sticking out near the doorway. She was sitting slumped down on the old sofa, and he thought she was asleep with a brown paper bag over her head. She took the bag off when he came in. She said, "What do you do for the hiccups? I heard—*whoop!* Excuse me—you put a bag on your head. Did you ever hear of that?"

"It's a carbon dioxide signal," he said. "It tells the brain to stop. I forget what. Carbon dioxide. I know that part of it."

"So I'm right to do this?"

He shrugged.

"Okay," she said. She put the bag back over her head and sat up straighter. "Have a seat."

Pete sat down on her desk chair and looked up her skirt. The beginnings of her thighs were long. There

was something terrific about long muscles like that.
Her head was in the brown wrinkled bag, but he felt
he had to look anyhow. He asked, "How's life?"

"I'm having fun," she said. "How's Pete?"

"Dynamite," he said.

She said, "Bang." She took the bag off her head and
shook her hair. It was short and light brown. If you
held a jar of honey up to the light in the Great American market, it was the same color as Miz Bean's hair.
She pinched the bag and blew into it. When it was
full, she hiccuped. Then she punched the bag, and it
exploded. He jumped and got mad. She said, "Dynamite." She hiccuped again.

Pete said, "You're supposed to scare yourself, not
me."

"Why?"

"Then you get rid of the hiccups."

"Ah. Well, *did* I scare you?"

"No."

"Oh. Well, how do you suppose somebody would
be able to scare herself?"

"Easy," he said.

"How?"

"I don't know. But easy. You know. Tell yourself
something bad or something."

"But wouldn't I know it was coming? Wouldn't I
know what I was going to tell myself?"

He said, "Sometimes it doesn't matter. Sometimes
you can still sneak up on yourself."

"How would *you* do it, Pete?"

"I'll think about it and I'll let you know."

"Okay. But, anyway, I think I stopped my hiccups. Don't tell me, though. They might start up."

"How'd you stop?"

"Just sitting here and talking to you." She was smiling, but she didn't look happy. She didn't seem to be a person who was talking about the hiccups.

"Maybe I'm something scary," he said.

She nodded. She looked like she was going to cry. One minute she was joking and making bags explode, and the next she looked red and upset. He was getting nervous.

She was watching him watch her, and he stood up to leave. She said, "Close the door, please, would you? And sit down for a minute?"

He shut the door. He sat down to wait. Part of what he did every day was look for clues. He thought he might figure out why she left them behind. Why she left him.

Miz Bean said, "I got a phone call from a friend of mine. She's adopting a baby, she and her husband."

Pete said, "That's cool enough." He nodded.

"She and I went to graduate school together. She's as old as I am."

"You're thirty-four."

"What else do you hear around the house, Pete?"

"None of that stuff," he said.

"What stuff? None of *what*?"

"You know. Making out and everything."

"Adults don't make out, Pete."

"I'm not saying they do, Miz Bean."

She said, "I'm thirty-five. I had a birthday last week. That was when your father and I went out for a dreadful dinner that you didn't want to come to."

"There was a flick I wanted to watch on the tube."

"You were being nice to us. You don't have to admit it. Anyway. I told this to your father, and I'll tell it to you. This friend of mine . . ." This time one of the tears got out of her eye. He watched it. Then he looked someplace else. He heard her blow her nose. All of a sudden, her face looked chapped. In a gluey voice she said, "You come in here . . ." She cleared her throat and said, "You come in here. You tell me all kinds of things. You know: secrets."

He nodded.

"So this is about me," she said. "I'm giving it over, and you can do whatever you think you should do with it. I'd just as soon you held on to it. Your father knows. We're very fine friends, he and I. He has this, and you can too." She blew her nose again and said, "When I was a good deal younger, I got pregnant. I had a baby. A doctor who was a friend of mine helped me have the baby, and I couldn't take care of it. I was a little crazy, then. You know how that goes."

Pete said, "You got it adopted?"

She said, "I did. What do you think?"

"Good deal," he said. "Smart move." He didn't know. He thought it would make her feel better. Maybe it *was* a smart move. Except of course she was sitting there, crying. And he didn't like the idea of a mother giving her baby away.

Not that he was a baby, of course.

But what he said was nothing he expected to say. He heard himself ask her, "Miz Bean? Am I your kid?"

"Oh," she said. "Oh, darling Pete. Oh, sweetheart, wouldn't that be *perfect* for us?" She was crying harder now, and he couldn't look away. She blew her nose and rubbed her cheeks with her hands. She said, "No. No. I'm sorry. But no."

He said, "Should we check on it? Is there a way we could check?"

"No, darling."

"You're sure, huh?"

"I'm afraid I am."

"Yeah," he said.

"I'm sorry."

"Yeah."

She looked at him. He couldn't look back anymore. He said, "I have to go to class."

"Then open the door," she said. "Make your escape."

That afternoon, with Pop driving them home, Pete asked his father about the time he got the medal and his mother went to City Hall to see it pinned on the stiff blue uniform shirt. "I remember when you guys came home and you paid the baby-sitter and Mom started crying."

"Yes," his father said. He sounded unhappy.

Pete said, "She started hitting you. She said you didn't care if you died. She said people who didn't care if they died didn't love the people they were leaving behind. She said—"

"Come on. That's a lot of crap."

"It is?"

"Don't you think, really, I loved you and your mother?"

"You didn't love Mom. You don't."

"Not that simple."

"You did love her?"

"Not *that* simple."

"And me?"

"Simple."

"So people who don't care if they die do love some of the people they leave behind them?"

"Geez, Pete, *I* don't know. Look: If they love them, they love them. The dying doesn't mean that much, I guess."

"It doesn't?"

"I don't think that's true, what I said, kid. I think it does. The dying means a lot, maybe. Hey: Am I a philosopher here?"

"Which is it?" Pete asked. "Does it mean a lot or not?"

Pop shifted behind the wheel, and Pete heard his leather jacket creak. "I don't know," his father said. He sounded sad. His voice sounded small.

Pete said, "To tell you the truth, I don't, either."

That night, after dinner, Pop fell asleep on the sofa.

Then he woke up and made noises like somebody with his head under water. Then he turned his reading light out and he went upstairs. Then he woke up after midnight and he went to read awhile on the sofa in the TV room. Then he fell asleep. Pete lay in his bed with a book he wasn't reading, and he followed the sounds from room to room. Pop did this every night. Pete got out of bed and put his pants on over his pajamas. He went down, listening for his father's snores. Pete went into the pantry for the big blue lobster pot they never cooked in. He squatted, took the cover off, reached in, and unrolled the gray cloth. It felt heavy, even though it was small. He always thought that, how heavy it was. It was black, and it weighed down his hand. There was a lot of stuff concentrated in there, he thought. He had the cartridge in his jeans pocket. Pop kept the cartridges upstairs, away from the pistol, but Pete had sneaked one to keep in his underwear drawer. The gun didn't click out loud like the guns on TV. Everything it did was soft and sure and heavy. He pushed the slide and turned his hand, and the drum swung out sideways. It had six black empty holes, and they showed up quietly. He dropped the cartridge into one of them and pushed it with his thumb.

In his bare feet he went outside. He carried the gun with the cylinder still lying sideways to the rest of it. He went across the road and over the fence and up their hill. They had moved there four months before, and Pop had never climbed up onto the land he owned. He looked at maps and read books and

watched some sports on TV and he fell asleep. Pete
wondered if his father ever got laid. He thought of Miz
Bean and his father. He hoped that old guys didn't
whack off, but he wasn't sure. The grass was cold. The
weather was changing. There was fog up on the hill. It
was blowing away. He was beginning to make out the
stars. About two hundred trillion insects kept making
the same one noise. It was like standing next to the
ocean at Riis Park. The same owl that lived in what
was supposed to be a butternut tree made the same
noises it made every night. It gave Pete the same feeling. The owl sounded like an old man right next to
him who was trying to frighten him. It was wet between his toes now. He had to lean into the hill to
keep his balance. After a while he was up. He was
breathing hard. He hadn't thought the hill was *that*
steep.

So here it is. He's sitting on the hillside while the
fog blows off, and he looks at the sky. The patterns of
the stars confuse him. He doesn't see them as archers
and sisters and bulls. The stars look to him like a mess.
He tries to think of something he could think about.
He keeps waiting for something important. The air is
wet. It touches his cheek like a hand. When his
mother left the custody hearing, she did that. She did
it with the ends of her fingers. He remembers that he
closed his eyes, and when he opened them, he saw that
his mother's eyes were closed. He breathes in the fog as
it whispers away. It doesn't taste like anything except
cold.

He's on the hill outside their house. He looks at the house like he's looking at their lives. He closes the gun. It makes a low locking sound. He spins the chambers of the cylinder. They don't spin terribly far around. He does it again and then once more. The cylinder is heavy, and it gives him the feeling of a big machine moving. He puts the gun in his mouth, and he gags on it. Then he pushes the trigger with his thumb. It doesn't feel right with his thumb. He puts his index finger into the guard and squeezes off and absolutely nothing happens.

He takes the gun out and wipes the wet barrel on his pajama tops. He is about to put it in his mouth again when he remembers that he might have forgotten to spin the cylinder. That cuts your odds down, he thinks. Or does it? He's terrible in math. Maybe it helps your odds. You have to know what you want to happen before you can think about odds, he figures.

He thinks about Miz Bean and her baby, about Pop and Miz Bean. He thinks about his mother and himself. Lights are going on upstairs in the house. He doesn't hear his father's voice, but he knows his father is calling for him. Pete knows about the feeling of the pistol in his mouth. He thinks he tried to fire the gun. He isn't sure, but he thinks so. Now the lights are on downstairs. The house looks far away, and Pete feels like somebody else on a hill across the road from the home of strangers in the middle of the night.

Finally the front porch light goes on. Finally his father in his white terry-cloth robe and plaid pajamas with his bare feet squeezed into his school shoes is standing on the porch. He shouts out Pete's name. He whispers "Damn" to himself. "Pete!" he hollers.

Pete can lie flat. Or he can stand up. Or he can crawl away and be hidden by brush. He can put the pistol in his mouth again and make sure he really tries to fire a round. It isn't that hard, he thinks.

His father holds his arms across his chest like he's hanging on. It was the way Pete's mother stood when the kids from Avenue U chased him home. Pop squints through the light on the porch and says, "Pete?"

His father steps off the porch and goes to the end of the walk, then into the road. He stands in it, hugging himself, looking up the hill. He says, "Pete? Is that you?"

His father takes a step, then stops. He whispers to himself, not to Pete. But Pete hears what he says.

His father whispers, "Please."

Okay, Pete says to himself. He stands up. He begins to walk down the hill. It happens as easy as that. Okay.

He walks over the cold grass and damp earth toward their house. He checks with his fingers to be certain the drum is out. He opens the gun out and holds it over his head. He walks with his hands in the air so his father can tell he's coming to give himself up.

For Ben and Nick

FREDERICK BUSCH is a much-acclaimed adult fiction writer with twenty published books to his credit, including *The Children in the Woods, Long Way from Home, Closing Arguments, Harry and Catherine,* and *Girls.* He has received a PEN/Malamud Award in short fiction, an award for fiction from the American Academy of Arts and Letters, a National Jewish Book Award, and Guggenheim and NEA fellowships, and has been nominated for the PEN/Faulkner Award.

"The story 'Custody,' " he says, "is based on a scene in my novel *Sometimes I Live in the Country.* A boy from New York City is spirited upstate by his father, who is enmeshed in an ugly divorce and custody suit. Because his father was a policeman, a gun is in the house and available to the boy. My wife and I came from the New York metropolitan area to upstate New York, and soon there were two boys in the house. I have read enough to be convinced that when a gun is available, in times of stress it will very likely be used. For that reason, we never owned a gun: We were frightened for our children's lives."

SHOTGUN CHEATHAM'S LAST NIGHT ABOVE GROUND

by Richard Peck

The first time I ever saw a dead body, it was Shotgun Cheatham. We were staying with our Grandma Dowdel, and it was the best trip by far we ever made to her house. My sister Mary Alice and I visited at Grandma Dowdel's every summer when our folks went up to fish in Wisconsin on Dad's week off.

"They dump us on her is what they do," Mary Alice said. She'd have been about nine the year they buried Shotgun. She didn't like going to Grandma's because you had to go outside to the privy. A big old snaggle-toothed tomcat lived in the cobhouse, and as quick as you'd come out of the privy, he'd jump at you. Mary Alice hated that.

I liked going to Grandma's because we went on the train. You could go just about anywhere on a train in those days, and I didn't care where a train went as long as I was on it. The tracks cut through the town where Grandma Dowdel lived, and people stood out on their porches to see the train go through. It was a town that size.

Mary Alice said there was nothing to do and nobody to do it with, so she'd tag after me, though I was three years older and a boy. We'd stroll uptown, which was three brick buildings: the bank, the general merchandise, and The Coffee Pot Cafe where the old saloon had stood. Prohibition was on in those days, so people made beer at home. They still had the tin roofs out over the sidewalk and hitching rails. Most farmers came to town horse-drawn, though there were Fords, and the banker drove a Hupmobile.

But it was a slow place except for the time they buried Shotgun Cheatham. He might have made it unnoticed all the way to the grave except for his name. The county seat newspaper didn't want to run an obituary on anybody called Shotgun, but nobody knew any other name for him. This sparked attention from some of the bigger newspapers. One sent in a stringer to nose around The Coffee Pot Cafe for a human-interest story since it was August, a slow month for news.

The Coffee Pot was where people went to loaf, talk tall, and swap gossip. Mary Alice and I were regulars there, and even we were of some interest because we were kin of Mrs. Dowdel's who never set foot in the place. She kept herself to herself, which was uphill work in a town like that.

Mary Alice and I carried the tale home that a suspicious type had come off the train in citified clothes and a stiff straw hat. He stuck out a mile and was asking around about Shotgun Cheatham. And he was taking notes.

Grandma had already heard it on the grapevine that Shotgun was no more, though she wasn't the first person people ran to with news. She wasn't what you'd call a popular woman. Grandpa Dowdel had been well thought of, but he was long gone.

That day she was working tomatoes on the black iron range, and her kitchen was hot enough to steam the calendars off the wall. Her sleeves were turned back, and she had arms on her like a man. When she heard the town was apt to fill up with newspaper reporters, her jaw clenched.

Presently she said, "I'll tell you what that reporter's after. He wants to get the horselaugh on us because he thinks we're nothing but a bunch of hayseeds and no-'count country people. We are, but what business is it of his?"

"Who was Shotgun Cheatham anyway?" Mary Alice asked.

"He was just an old reprobate who lived poor and died broke," Grandma said. "Nobody went near him because he smelled like a polecat. He lived in a chicken coop, and now they'll have to burn it down."

To change the subject she said to me, "Here, you stir these tomatoes, and don't let them stick. I've stood in this heat till I'm half-cooked myself."

I hated it when Grandma gave me kitchen work. I wished it was her day for apple butter. She made that outdoors over an open fire, and she put pennies in the caldron to keep it from sticking.

"Down at The Coffee Pot they say Shotgun rode with the James boys."

"Which James boys?" Grandma asked.

"Jesse James," I said, "and Frank."

"They wouldn't have had him," she said. "Anyhow, those Jameses were Missouri people."

"They were telling the reporter Shotgun killed a man and went to the penitentiary."

"Several around here done that," Grandma said, "though I don't recall him being out of town any length of time. Who's doing all this talking?"

"A real old, humped-over lady with buck teeth," Mary Alice said.

"Cross-eyed?" Grandma said. "That'd be Effie Wilcox. You think she's ugly now, you should have seen her as a girl. And she'd talk you to death. Her tongue's attached in the middle and flaps at both ends." Grandma was over by the screen door for a breath of air.

"They said he'd notched his gun in six places," I said, pushing my luck. "They said the notches were either for banks he'd robbed or for sheriffs he'd shot."

"Was that Effie again? Never trust an ugly woman. She's got a grudge against the world," said Grandma, who was no oil painting herself. She fetched up a sigh. "I'll tell you how Shotgun got his name. He wasn't but about ten years old, and he wanted to go out and shoot quail with a bunch of older boys. He couldn't

hit a barn wall from the inside, and he had a sty in one
eye. They were out there in a pasture without a quail
in sight, but Shotgun got all excited being with the big
boys. He squeezed off a round and killed a cow. Down
she went. If he'd been aiming at her, she'd have died of
old age eventually. The boys took the gun off him, not
knowing who he'd plug next. That's how he got the
name, and it stuck to him like flypaper. Any girl in
town could have outshot him, and that includes me."
Grandma jerked a thumb at herself.

She kept a twelve-gauge double-barreled Winchester
Model 21 behind the woodbox, but we figured it had
been Grandpa Dowdel's for shooting ducks. "And I
wasn't no Annie Oakley myself, except with squirrels."
Grandma was still at the door, fanning her apron.
Then in the same voice she said, "Looks like we got
company. Take them tomatoes off the fire."

A stranger was on the porch, and when Mary Alice
and I crowded up behind Grandma to see, it was the
reporter. He was sharp-faced, and he'd sweated
through his hatband.

"What's your business?" Grandma said through
screen wire, which was as friendly as she got.

"Ma'am, I'm making inquiries about the late Shotgun Cheatham." He shuffled his feet, wanting to get
one of them in the door. Then he mopped up under
his hat brim with a silk handkerchief. His Masonic
ring had diamond chips in it.

"Who sent you to me?"

"I'm going door-to-door, ma'am. You know how

you ladies like to talk. Bless your hearts, you'd all talk the hind leg off a mule."

Mary Alice and I both stared at that. We figured Grandma would grab up her broom to swat him off the porch. She could make short work of peddlers even when they weren't lippy. And tramps never marked her fence. But to our surprise she swept open the screen door and stepped out on the back porch. You didn't get inside her house even if you knew her. I followed and so did Mary Alice once she was sure the snaggle-toothed tom wasn't lurking around out there, waiting to pounce.

"You a newspaper reporter?" she said. "Peoria?" It was the flashy clothes, but he looked surprised. "What they been telling you?"

"Looks like I got a good story by the tail," he said. " 'Last of the Old Owlhoot Gunslingers Goes to a Pauper's Grave.' That kind of angle. Ma'am, I wonder if you could help me flesh out the story some."

"Well, I got flesh to spare," Grandma said mildly. "Who's been talking to you?"

"It was mainly an elderly lady—"

"Ugly as sin, calls herself Wilcox?" Grandma said. "She's been in the state hospital for the insane until just here lately, but as a reporter I guess you nosed that out."

Mary Alice nudged me hard, and the reporter's eyes widened.

"They tell you how Shotgun come by his name?"

"Opinions seem to vary, ma'am."

"Ah well, fame is fleeting," Grandma said. "He got it in the Civil War."

The reporter's hand hovered over his breast pocket where a notepad stuck out.

"Oh yes, Shotgun went right through the war with the Illinois Volunteers. Shiloh in the spring of sixty-two, and he was with U. S. Grant when Vicksburg fell. That's where he got his name. Grant give it to him, in fact. Shotgun didn't hold with government-issue fire-arms. He shot rebels with his old Remington pump-action that he'd used to kill quail back here at home."

Now Mary Alice was yanking on my shirttail. We knew kids lie all the time, but Grandma was no kid, and she could tell some whoppers. Of course the reporter had been lied to big-time up at the cafe, but Grandma's lies were more interesting, even historical. They made Shotgun look better while they left Effie Wilcox in the dust.

"He was always a crack shot," she said, winding down. "Come home from the war with a line of medals bigger than his chest."

"And yet he died penniless," the reporter said in a thoughtful voice.

"Oh well, he'd sold off them medals and give the money to war widows and orphans."

A change crossed the reporter's narrow face. Shotgun had gone from kill-crazy gunslinger to war hero marksman. Philanthropist, even. He fumbled his note-pad out and was scribbling. He thought he'd hit pay dirt with Grandma. "It's all a matter of record," she said. "You could look it up."

He was ready to wire in a new story: "Civil War Hero Handpicked by U. S. Grant called to the Great Campground in the Sky." Something like that. "And he never married?"

"Never did," Grandma said. "He broke Effie Wilcox's heart. She's bitter still, as you see."

"And now he goes to a pauper's grave with none to mark his passing," the reporter said, which may have been a sample of his writing style.

"They tell you that?" Grandma said. "They're pulling your leg, sonny. You drop by The Coffee Pot and tell them you heard that Shotgun's being buried from my house with full honors. He'll spend his last night above ground in my front room, and you're invited."

The reporter backed down the porch stairs, staggering under all this new material. "Much obliged, ma'am," he said.

"Happy to help," Grandma said.

Mary Alice had turned loose of my shirttail. What little we knew about grown-ups never seemed to cover Grandma. She turned on us. "Now I've got to change my shoes and walk all the way up to the lumberyard in this heat," she said, as if she hadn't brought it all on herself. Up at the lumberyard they'd be knocking together Shotgun Cheatham's coffin and sending the bill to the county, and Grandma had to tell them to bring that coffin to her house, with Shotgun in it.

*   *   *

By nightfall a green pine coffin stood on two sawhorses
in the bay window of the front room, and people
milled in the yard. They couldn't see Shotgun from
there because the coffin lid blocked the view. Besides,
a heavy gauze hung from the open lid and down over
the front of the coffin to veil him. Shotgun hadn't
been exactly fresh when they discovered his body.
Grandma had flung open every window, but there was
a peculiar smell in the room. I'd only had one look at
him when they'd carried in the coffin, and that was
enough. I'll tell you just two things about him. He
didn't have his teeth in, and he was wearing bib over-
alls.

The people in the yard still couldn't believe
Grandma was holding open house. This didn't stop
the reporter who was haunting the parlor, looking for
more flesh to add to his story. And it didn't stop Mrs.
L. J. Weidenbach, the banker's wife, who came leading
her father, an ancient codger half her size in full Civil
War Union blue.

"We are here to pay our respects at this sad time,"
Mrs. Weidenbach said when Grandma let them in.
"When I told Daddy that Shotgun had been decorated
by U. S. Grant and wounded three times at Bull Run,
it brought it all back to him, and we had to come."
Her old daddy wore a forage cap and a decoration
from the Grand Army of the Republic, and he seemed
to have no idea where he was. She led him up to the

coffin, where they admired the flowers. Grandma had planted a pitcher of glads from her garden at either end of the pine box. In each pitcher she'd stuck an American flag.

A few more people willing to brave Grandma came and went, but finally we were down to the reporter who'd settled into the best chair, still nosing for news. Then who appeared at the front door but Mrs. Effie Wilcox, in a hat.

"Mrs. Dowdel, I've come to set with you overnight and see our brave old soldier through his Last Watch."

In those days people sat up with a corpse through the final night before burial. I'd have bet money Grandma wouldn't let Mrs. Wilcox in for a quick look, let alone overnight. But of course Grandma was putting on the best show possible to pull wool over the reporter's eyes. Little though she thought of towns-people, she thought less of strangers. Grandma waved Mrs. Wilcox inside, and in she came, her eyes all over the place. She made for the coffin, stared at the blank white gauze, and said, "Don't he look natural?"

Then she drew up a chair next to the reporter. He flinched because he had it on good authority that she'd just been let out of an insane asylum. "Warm, ain't it?" she said straight at him, but looking everywhere.

The crowd outside finally dispersed. Mary Alice and I hung at the edge of the room, too curious to be anywhere else.

"If you're here for the long haul," Grandma said to the reporter, "how about a beer?" He looked encouraged, and Grandma left him to Mrs. Wilcox, which was meant as a punishment. She came back with three of her home brews, cellar-cool. She brewed beer to drink herself, but these three bottles were to see the reporter through the night. She wouldn't have expected her worst enemy, Effie Wilcox, to drink alcohol in front of a man.

In normal circumstances the family recalls stories about the departed to pass the long night hours. But these circumstances weren't normal, and quite a bit had already been recalled about Shotgun Cheatham anyway.

Only a single lamp burned, and as midnight drew on, the glads drooped in their pitchers. I was wedged in a corner, beginning to doze, and Mary Alice was sound asleep on a throw rug. After the second beer, the reporter lolled, visions of Shotgun's Civil War glories no doubt dancing in his head. You could hear the tick of the kitchen clock. Grandma's chin would drop, then jerk back. Mrs. Wilcox had been humming "Rock of Ages," but tapered off after "let me hide myself in thee."

Then there was the quietest sound you ever heard. Somewhere between a rustle and a whisper. It brought me around, and I saw Grandma sit forward and cock her head. I blinked to make sure I was awake, and the whole world seemed to listen. Not a leaf trembled outside.

But the gauze that hung down over the open coffin moved. Twitched.

Except for Mary Alice, we all saw it. The reporter sat bolt upright, and Mrs. Wilcox made a little sound.

Then nothing.

Then the gauze rippled as if a hand had passed across it from the other side, and in one place it wrinkled into a wad as if somebody had snagged it. As if a feeble hand had reached up from the coffin depths in one last desperate attempt to live before the dirt was shoveled in.

Every hair on my head stood up.

"Naw," Mrs. Wilcox said, strangling. She pulled back in her chair, and her hat went forward. "Naw!"

The reporter had his chair arms in a death grip. "Sweet mother of—"

But Grandma rocketed out of her chair. "Whoa, Shotgun!" she bellowed. "You've had your time, boy. You don't get no more!"

She galloped out of the room faster than I'd ever seen her move. The reporter was riveted, and Mrs. Wilcox was sinking fast.

Quicker than it takes to tell, Grandma was back and already raised to her aproned shoulder was the twelve-gauge Winchester from behind the woodbox. She swung it wildly around the room, skimming Mrs. Wilcox's hat, and took aim at the gauze that draped the yawning coffin. Then she squeezed off a round.

I thought that sound would bring the house down. I couldn't hear right for a week. Then Grandma roared out, "Rest in peace, I tell you, you old—" Then she let fly with the other barrel.

The reporter came out of the chair and whipped completely around in a circle. Beer bottles went everywhere. The straight route to the front door was in Grandma's line of fire, and he didn't have the presence of mind to realize she'd already discharged both barrels. He went out a side window, headfirst, leaving his hat and his notepad behind. Which he feared more, the living dead or Grandma's aim, he didn't tarry to tell. Mrs. Wilcox was on her feet, hollering, "The dead is walking, and Mrs. Dowdel's gunning for me!" She cut and ran out the door and into the night.

When the screen door snapped to behind her, silence fell. Mary Alice hadn't moved. The first explosion had blasted her awake, but she naturally thought that Grandma had killed her, so she didn't bother to budge. She says the whole experience gave her nightmares for years after.

A burned-powder haze hung in the room, cutting the smell of Shotgun Cheatham. The white gauze was black rags now, and Grandma had blown the lid clear off the coffin. She'd have blown out all three windows in the bay, except they were open. As it was, she'd pitted her woodwork bad and topped the snowball bushes outside. But apart from scattered shot, she hadn't disfigured Shotgun Cheatham any more than he already was.

Grandma stood there savoring the silence. Then she turned toward the kitchen with the twelve-gauge loose in her hand. "Time you kids was in bed," she said as she trudged past us.

Apart from Grandma herself, I was the only one who'd seen her big old snaggle-toothed tomcat streak out of the coffin and over the windowsill when she let fire. And I supposed she'd seen him climb in, which gave her ideas. It was the cat, sitting smug on Shotgun Cheatham's breathless chest, who'd batted at the gauze the way a cat will. And he sure lit out the way he'd come when Grandma fired just over his ragged ears, as he'd probably used up eight lives already.

The cat in the coffin gave Grandma Dowdel her chance. She never had any time for Effie Wilcox, whose tongue flapped at both ends, but she had even less for newspaper reporters who think your business is theirs. Courtesy of the cat, she'd fired a round, so to speak, in the direction of each.

Though she never gloated, she looked satisfied. It certainly fleshed out her reputation and gave people new reason to leave her in peace. The story of Shotgun Cheatham's last night above ground kept The Coffee Pot Cafe fully engaged for the rest of that long summer. It was a story that grew in the telling in one of those little towns where there's always time to ponder all the different kinds of truth.

RICHARD PECK has received the Margaret A. Edwards Award for lifetime achievement in young adult literature. He is the author of more than twenty books for teenagers, including *Are You in the House Alone?* and *Dreamland Lake* (both winners of the Edgar Allan Poe Award for mystery writers), *Remembering the Good Times, Unfinished Portrait of Jessica, Bel-Air Bambi and the Mall Rats, The Last Safe Place on Earth,* and *Lost in Cyberspace.*

He writes, "My father had come of age, or lost his youth, on the French battlefields of World War One, and the war's evidence lay all around my childhood. A Luger pistol my dad took off a dead German lived in the top drawer of a bureau. His American guns, shotguns for pheasant and quail season, stood behind the refrigerator. He illegally fired off a couple of barrels only once within the city limits, on the day the Second World War was over.

"My own history with guns began and ended on the firing range at Fort Carson, Colorado, when I qualified on an M-1 rifle, and then spent the rest of an army career ghostwriting sermons for chaplains. And so for 'Shotgun Cheatham's Last Night Above Ground,' I harked back to my dad's memories of the country town where he grew up and where my grandmother still lived when I was a kid.

"Was Grandma Dowdel my own grandmother? No, though there's a physical resemblance. My grandmother would neither have brewed nor drunk beer, and she commanded a different kind of respect from her neighbors. But the house was hers, the calendars in the kitchen, the bay window and the snowball bushes, the privy at the end of the garden, opposite the cobhouse. The settings of writers' childhoods always seem to find their ways into our stories."

THE WAR CHEST

by Rob Thomas

The old man didn't like talking. At least not about stuff old men are supposed to like talking about. You know, about the good old days—when movies cost a nickel, slow dancing had real steps, and the scariest gang members carried switchblades.

What he *did* like was TV. Unfortunately for both of us, the forty-five minutes I was supposed to entertain him after basketball practice every Monday, Wednesday, and Friday coincided with *Jeopardy!* I don't know if it was his favorite show, but he must have liked it a lot, because he'd glare at me if I tried to say anything while it was on.

Everyone who graduates from Lee High School, including yours truly, has to complete two hundred hours of community service. That's the bad news. The good news is that they're pretty flexible about how you get those hours. There's a two-page list up in Mrs. Everett's room of all the choices: suicide hotlines, soup kitchens, churches, hospitals. I chose the Grandfriends program. That's the one where they pair you up with a resident of the Regency Gardens Retirement Community. I chose Grandfriends, I guess, because none of my real grandparents are still alive. Mom said I needed to be around old folks or I'd end up like one of those teenage guys who gets his kicks plowing his four-by-four through their dahlia patches or wrapping their little rat dogs in duct tape.

When we signed up as Grandfriends, the people at Regency Gardens hooked us up with the residents who rarely received visitors. Mr. Owens, the chief administrator, explained this practice to us in an orientation session.

"Their families, for whatever reason—proximity, time constraints—aren't able to come by that often," he said. "And a lot of our patients have outlived their friends."

With the other Grandfriends, what Mr. Owens said was probably true. In Mr. Conradt's case, I think isolation was a lifestyle choice.

The first day I visited his room, I figured it might be awkward, so I made a mental list of things to talk about, just to try to get the ball rolling. I asked him if he liked fishing. He sneered. I asked him if he had traveled much. He stared at the TV. I asked him if he liked basketball. Mr. Conradt hawked up some phlegm.

The television in Mr. Conradt's room was mounted high in a corner, and the padded office-style chairs we

sat in were aimed in that direction. The walls of the
room had been painted eggshell white, and the twelve-
by-twelve space was lit by a half dozen fluorescent
tubes—five more than the square footage required.
The quasi-supernova glare washed the color out of everything within. I squinted on my first day as I
scanned the old man's chambers for anything I could
use to strike up a conversation—golf tees, books, post-
cards. Nothing. A *TV Guide* was the closest thing I
could find to a memento.

"What did you used to do?" I asked. "Before you
retired."

The Final Jeopardy music played while Mr. Conradt
ignored my question.

"Who is Tito," he said. So did an attorney from Del
Mar, California, who ended up sixteen hundred dollars richer as a result. When they cut to a commercial,
the old man spoke.

"I know the score," he said. "I know it better than
you. I know why you're here. It's because you have to
be and because it looked like the easiest job on some
list. You thought you'd come down here and brighten
up a sad old man's day. And that maybe he'd want to
teach you how to tie flies or build a box kite."

He leaned closer, but I couldn't look him in the eye.
I stared at the brown splotches on his forehead and
inhaled the powerful fumes of cologne swirling like fog
around him. He wasn't as tall as me, but his shoulders
were as wide, which is saying something—I set the
best picks in the district.

"Well, I'll make you a deal," Mr. Conradt said. "You sit here and keep your mouth shut, and I'll return the favor. You won't have to hear what's wrong with kids today, or about my latest operation, or about the best ear of corn I ever ate."

Vanna White appeared on the TV screen, and Mr. Conradt seemed to lose his fire as *Wheel of Fortune* sucked him in. That was fine with me; I didn't know how to respond to his offer.

The next few times that I went to see Mr. Conradt, we didn't talk at all except during the first commercial break, when he'd tell me—without offering me any change for the machine—that he wanted a Dr Pepper. I'd go get him one, and he'd grunt as he accepted the drink from me. When I passed in front of him to get back to my chair, he'd panic—lean over, nearly fall out of his chair—during the split second I blocked his view of the television.

It was probably during my third week on the job that I arrived at Regency Gardens in time to watch a nurse tend to Mr. Conradt. He was bent over the edge of his bed, and his dark slacks were down around his ankles. At first I thought it was strange that he wasn't wearing boxers—you just expect old men to wear boxers—but on second glance I understood why he wasn't. He was wearing those diapers they make for adults. If I'd thought the old man saved all his hostility for me, the scene purged me of that self-important theory. He glared at the nurse with such blatant loathing that I thought she'd

spontaneously burst into flames. She was trying hard
to be nice, but everything she said or did just made
Mr. Conradt angrier. He spotted me in the room
while the nurse was applying some sort of lotion or
cream to his thick, yellowish legs. He responded
with an inventory of curse words that managed to
embarrass me and rid the nurse of any remaining
bedside manner. She checked his blood pressure
without allowing him to pull up his pants.

Before she left his room, the nurse gathered a number of pills from her cart and handed them to Mr.
Conradt in a paper container. She stepped into his
bathroom to pour him some water, but Mr. Conradt
swallowed the pills, then refused the Dixie cup she
offered.

We didn't watch TV that day. We didn't talk either.
Mr. Conradt just sat in his chair clenching and un-
clenching his jaw. I pulled my Walkman out of my
backpack, slipped on the headphones, and silently
vowed that when I got that old, I wouldn't be like
Lester Conradt.

I talked to Mrs. Everett at school a few days later. I
asked her if it was too late to get a different assignment
and told her that I didn't care what it was.

"It can't be all that bad, Jeff," she said. "Just give it
a couple more weeks. If you still want to change after
that, I'll see what I can do."

So we kept at it. Mr. Conradt watched TV. I listened to my Walkman and did my homework.

I had stupidly signed up for Mr. Twilley's honors

American history class. Normally I'm a pretty decent student, but trying to take Twilley's class during basketball season was a big mistake. The man just assigns too much stuff. Too many pages to read. Too many questions to answer. Too many papers to write. On a Monday afternoon, I sat in Mr. Conradt's room and worked on chapter summary questions covering World War II. I saw Mr. Conradt's head spin around. He was mouthing something. I pulled off my earphones.

"What?"

"Nearly fifty thousand," he said. Apparently I had been reading the questions out loud. "Forty-eight to be exact. Forty-eight thousand Americans lost on Okinawa."

"Thanks," I said. I didn't know if I should trust his answer, though he was usually right on when he played along with *Jeopardy!* He saw me hesitate.

"I don't give a damn whether you believe it or not, just as long as you keep quiet. But I should know," he said. "I was there."

"Were you a Marine?" I asked, having just read that the marines did most of the fighting at Okinawa.

"What is Sanskrit," he said, his attention having returned to the television.

I tried again.

"My dad is a gun collector. Well, really, he's an antique dealer, but he's got lots of antique guns. A couple from World War Two."

No response. I moved ahead to the next question, but a couple minutes later, Mr. Conradt spoke.

"Read in the paper you had twelve rebounds last night."

"Just lucky, I guess."

"Naw, lucky is making all your free throws," Conradt said. "Rebounding—that's hustle and desire. How tall are you?"

"Six three."

"Now that's tall, but it's not *that* tall. Must be a hard worker."

And that's how we started talking. I mean, it didn't just happen all of a sudden; commenting on my basketball game sort of paved the way. Then he decided he wanted to hear about my dad's guns after all. He asked what models my dad kept.

"One's a Colt Browning. Pretty common. Dad says it's not worth much. But the other one is a Japanese pistol. A Hossenfeffer . . . Hit Parader . . . Hot Potato."

"Hamada," Mr. Conradt said.

"That's the one," I said. "You've seen them before?"

Instead of answering, Mr. Conradt gave me an order: "Go open up my closet and pull my chest out here."

I did as I was told. The chest was an antique. Green camouflage. Military.

"Open it up."

I flipped up the lid and got a quick look inside before Mr. Conradt had me slide it over to him. Everything I saw was old. The coolest thing was a bayonet, but I saw his dog tags lying on top of an old uniform.

"My dad would love to see all of this. Is it all World War Two stuff?"

"Yep," Mr. Conradt said as he reached beneath the clothes and pulled a Japanese helmet out from the bottom of the chest. "A Hamada was what this son of a bitch used on my sergeant before I dropped him."

Mr. Conradt handed me the helmet.

"Did he live?"

"You think he just gave me the helmet? I asked him real sweet and he handed it over for a souvenir?"

"I meant the sergeant."

"For about two hours. Gut wound. He was scream-ing. We all knew he wasn't gonna make it, but we were nothing but a bunch of chickenshit twenty-year-olds. None of us had the balls to do a thing about it."

Mr. Conradt took the helmet back from me, even though I was still looking at it.

"So how you gonna stop that monster they got playing center over in Liberty Valley?"

After a while, my conversations with Mr. Conradt began to extend beyond island-hopping in the Pacific and the need to box out on the weak side. He wouldn't tell me anything personal regarding his life, but he was plenty interested in the nitty-gritty of mine. He even had a favorite theme.

"Why don't you have a girlfriend?"

"Because," I said slowly, "well . . . look, I don't know. Hell, just look at me."

He shook his head and looked simultaneously in-credulous and exasperated. I always found it interesting that Mr. Conradt was dressed like he would be heading off to the office at any minute. The residents I passed in the hallways wore bathrobes or sweat suits. Mr. Conradt always had on dark slacks and a collared dress shirt and tie, though the tie was usually loosened.

"No need to curse," he said, oblivious to his hypocrisy. "You're no uglier than I was. Are you even trying?"

"No."

"Have your eye on anyone?"

"No."

"You do like girls, don't you?"

"Yeah!" I said, getting sort of mad. "But I can't help it if they don't like me!"

"It's all attitude. You keep thinking like that, and of course you'll never have a girlfriend."

"What about you?" I said, deciding to take the offensive. "Lots of ladies here at Regency Gardens. Doing any courtin'?"

But Mr. Conradt just went back into *Jeopardy!* world, and I never got an answer.

The next time I came over for a visit, Mr. Conradt started talking right away.

"It's too bad," he said. "Too bad for you boys today."

"What's too bad?"

"No wars for you," he said. "Not even a decent chance for one. Small wars are over in a few days. Big one'll be over in a few seconds, and all of us'll be dead."

What he was saying seemed so ridiculous that I wondered if he'd been off his medication.

"Why would I want an experience like that?" I asked. "Didn't you say forty-eight thousand men died at Okinawa?"

"But they died *for* something. Better than just dying. Men I fought with in the war—those are friends for life. And I don't just mean the ones in my squad. I mean all of 'em. We're all connected. We all went through the same hell. Take Charlie for instance."

"Who's Charlie?"

"Charlie Roberts. He's new. He's over in D wing. Now he did most of his fighting in France, half a world away from where I was, but he's only been here a few months and it's like we've known each other our whole lives."

D wing was where they kept the residents who needed the most medical attention. They didn't let the D wing residents have Grandfriends. I thought Charlie Roberts must be a great storyteller to get Mr. Conradt to forget about *Jeopardy!* for an afternoon. Then I realized I was jealous. And that embarrassed me.

Mr. Conradt shifted gears. "So, Jeff," he said, his eyes getting beady, "tell me about this girl you like."

"I never said anything about liking *a* girl. I just said I liked girls."

"Don't bullshit an old man, Jeffy Boy. What's her name?"

He clicked off the TV, and for what seemed like a

long time, the only sound in the room was the buzzing
of the fluorescent lights.

"Well?" Somehow he made one eyebrow arch.

"Jenny," I said. "Jenny Robinson."

I never should have told him. I kind of hoped it
would be the omega of the discussion. Instead, it became the alpha. He wanted to know everything about
her. Everything I said to her. Everything about the
Spring Turnabout Dance.

"Why don't you ask her?" he demanded, eighty
hours into my commitment. He used his favorite tone
of voice. The one that made everything he said sound
like it followed *"Listen here, ya dipshit . . ."*

"The whole point of the Turnabout Dance is that
girls ask guys," I said. "It's kind of the way girls let
guys know who they want to take them to prom."

"Does she come to your games?" he asked.

"Yeah, but . . ."

"Well, there you go."

"She has to. She's on dance team."

"You're hopeless," he said. "Plain hopeless."

The next time I saw him, Mr. Conradt was in his
usual postrubdown crappy mood. I could tell because
he wasn't muttering the questions that go with the
Jeopardy! answers, and he didn't touch his Dr Pepper.
We sat silently until the show was over. The first commercial that came on afterward was for McDonald's. It
was one I'd seen before, but I'd never really thought
about it. In it a spritely senior citizen walks down the
street, smiling and waving to the people he passes. He

enters a McDonald's, and you're supposed to think that he's going to order something. Instead he pulls off his jacket, and he's wearing a McDonald's uniform. Next thing you know, the old fella's manning the fry machine side by side with a clear-skinned teenager. Big smiles from everyone.

"I designed buildings."

"What?" I said. I glanced over at Mr. Conradt, who was glowering at the TV.

"Some of the biggest in the state. Tower of The Americas in San Antonio is mine. Built it for the world's fair. American Bank Building in Austin was the tallest in the city when we built it in sixty-four. Had my own firm. Twenty-two people working for me at one time."

"You want to do something else one of these days?" I asked.

"What, flip burgers? Maybe get a paper route?"

"No," I said, "I mean, do you want to do something other than watch *Jeopardy!* every time I come over? Go for a walk or something."

Mr. Conradt didn't speak for a minute. At first, I was sure he was trying to think of something mean to say, but that wasn't it at all.

"I'd like to see you play sometime. If you can arrange it."

"I'll ask if it's all right."

"Will Jenny Robinson be dancing?"

"Is that the real reason you want to come?"

"It'll be a bonus," he said.

Mr. Owens had no problem with Mr. Conradt's attending one of my home games as long as my parents picked him up and took him back to Regency Gardens. The student council was selling Rebel Pride sweatshirts at school. I bought one for Mr. Conradt, and he wore it to the game.

I didn't have an especially great outing—seven points, nine rebounds—but I did steal an in-bounds pass at the end of the game when we were only up by two. Afterward, I rode home with my parents, dropping Mr. Conradt off along the way.

"He certainly thinks the world of you," Mom said as we pulled away from the home.

"Mr. Conradt?"

"He couldn't quit talking about what a nice young man you are, and how much he looks forward to your visits."

"He couldn't?"

Then Dad spoke up. "Now tell us about this Jenny Robinson."

Miss Robinson remained the chief topic of conversation the next time I showed up at Regency Gardens.

"She's a cutie, all right," reported Mr. Conradt.

"I can't believe you told my parents. Now I've got all three of you giving me a hard time."

Mr. Conradt turned down the television, even though it was right in the middle of Double Jeopardy.

"I'll tell you Jeff, now that I've seen you play, and I've seen Miss Robinson, I just don't see any reason

why you don't ask her out. Does she have a boyfriend?"

"No."

"Well then—" he began, but I was tired of his tone.

"Well then what?" I said. "You act like she'll go out
with me just because I'm on the basketball team. I
wish that's the way it worked, but it's not."

Mr. Conradt shook his head. "I'm not saying she'll
go out with you. What I'm saying is you should ask
her out. Maybe she will say no. If she does, so what?
Life is short, Jeffy Boy." Mr. Conradt reached over
and grabbed a bit of skin under my biceps and
pinched it. I guess he was checking to make sure I was
paying attention.

"Get out the war chest," he said with his usual
warmth.

I pulled it out of the closet and opened the lid. Mr.
Conradt withdrew the small metal box I had seen before. He yanked the lock open, then reached inside. I
couldn't see what he was getting until he pulled it all
the way out. It was a black-and-white photograph. He
handed it to me.

"Now—do you see one good reason why that girl
there would have ever wanted to give me the time of
day?"

I took a look at the woman in the photo. Her hair
was dark and luxuriously thick, and she had these great
big eyes and mischievous sexy smile. She was reclining
in some kind of deck chair, and you could see a long

stretch of sensational legs. Then I looked back up at
Mr. Conradt. At his round head and flat face. I
couldn't imagine him as handsome, even in his prime.

"No," I said.

He laughed. "If I hadn't worked up my nerve, there
never would have been a Mrs. Lester Conradt, and I
wouldn't have had that picture reminding me of why I
wanted to go home so bad."

I looked at the photo again and was, for the second
time, amazed that Mr. Conradt had landed such a
beautiful woman. If Lester the Detester could get himself a girl, so could I.

"You've got things to offer a young lady," Mr. Conradt said as I continued staring at the photo. "Now,
you're never going to be a movie star, but you're a
hard worker, and I don't just mean on the basketball
court. You study hard. And you're a good kid. I don't
know if anyone told you, but I've had two other
Grandfriends, and they've both thrown in the towel
after a couple weeks. You've really stuck it out. I know
I can be a pain in the backside."

"You think?" I said.

I doubt he knew I was being facetious.

More and more often when I showed up at Regency
Gardens, Mr. Conradt wouldn't be in his room. A
couple times he didn't even show up before it was my
time to leave. I knew where he was, though. He was
somewhere in D wing playing soldier with his one and
only friend, Charlie Roberts. Unless he considered me

a friend. Which was weird for me to think about. I mean I'd hated coming out to Regency Gardens at first, and here I was, telling my best-kept secrets to an eighty-year-old man. And he really seemed to get off on it too—teasing me, telling war stories, following the team. I was anxious to find him that particular Wednesday, because I knew what we'd talk about. I'd had a career-high seventeen points the night before. Instead of waiting around, I decided to track him. Leaving his room, I followed the brightly lit corridors, which reminded me, as usual, of elementary-school hallways. Colorful bulletin boards. Drinking fountains two and a half feet off the ground. The smell of cafeteria food in the distance. But the atmosphere changed when I made the left turn into D wing. Suddenly I felt like I had entered a hospital. The nurses who moved through these hallways smiled less and scurried more. The smell of turkey tetrazzini was wiped out by the pungency of rubbing alcohol. The only residents I saw were in wheelchairs.

I decided my scoring flurry wasn't such big news, but right when I was going to turn around and head back to wait in Mr. Conradt's room, I spied the door with Mr. Roberts's name on it. I approached it, though I was, as yet, undecided about whether I wanted to knock. I didn't have to. Right when I got there, the door eased open and Mr. Conradt stepped out into the hall, nearly bumping into me. My appearance pissed him off.

"What the hell are you doing down here?" he demanded.

I was about to tell him that I wanted to meet his friend and that I was anxious to talk about the game, but what I heard coming out of the room stopped me from explaining. Whoever was in there—I assumed it was Mr. Roberts—was ranting at full volume. Even though the door was shut, I could hear him clearly.

"Who said you could borrow my car? It's my car! Who said you could borrow my car?"

Then there came sobbing. Wailing, really.

The nurses and attendants walking through the hallways didn't even appear to notice the commotion. Mr. Conradt grabbed the arm of a blond nurse pushing a medicine cart.

"Are you deaf?" he said.

The nurse calmly called for an orderly—for Mr. Conradt, not for Mr. Roberts.

I said, "Come on, Mr. Conradt. Let me walk you back."

He let go of the nurse's arm and followed me reluctantly out of D wing.

That week I got asked to the Spring Turnabout Dance. Not by Jenny Robinson, though.

Laura Albertson, this girl I've been in a hundred classes with since eighth grade because we're both "college track," asked me. I stammered a bit, and I'm sure she thought I was going to say no, but I was just so shocked, you know, and believe it or not, I had to work up my nerve to say yes. It's funny she asked me. I

mean, I'd never really thought much about her. She's
nice and all, but I didn't even think she went to the
basketball games. We had a pretty good time at the
dance. I didn't fall in love or anything, but it was good
to see I could make it through it. I looked all around
at the dance, but I didn't see Jenny. That made me
happy, too.

After the event, Mr. Conradt expected a full report.

"Did you get any?"

That was his first question.

"Grow up," I said.

"So you didn't."

Only thirty hours and thirty minutes to go, I thought,
though really, I didn't mind the hours I spent down at
Regency Gardens anymore. Unless he had just come
from seeing Mr. Roberts, Mr. Conradt didn't even
have the TV on when I came over. He was having too
good a time harassing me or playing show-and-tell
with items from his war chest: his discharge papers, an
untouched rations kit, a volcanic rock that he said he
found on one of the islands where he fought. He was
in the middle of one of his favorite stories—hitting the
beach at Guadalcanal—when he brought up my dad's
guns.

"You think he'd let you show them to me? I haven't
seen one of those Hamadas in fifty years."

"No problem," I said.

I didn't even ask Dad, not that I thought I was
getting away with anything, but I knew he wouldn't
care. It's not like the guns were loaded. He bought and

sold antiques on weekends at flea markets and antique shows. It was a hobby at one point, but it had grown into a fairly profitable sideline for him. He was much more dedicated to it than to his administrative job at the Deerfield Water Treatment Facility. The problem with his obsession, as far as I was concerned, is that it turned our house into a shrine. Ever try having fun in a shrine? Don't run. Don't set your drink there. Don't sit in that chair. The guns were the only two antiques I ever had any fun with. Tevin Brown and I used to take them out and play gangsters with them. Last year a few of us videotaped ourselves acting out that John Woo movie *Hard Boiled.* I snuck the guns out for that too.

The day I took the pistols to Mr. Conradt was a blast. He just lit up. I probably sat in his room for three hours while he picked imaginary snipers out of trees as he told war stories. He talked about all the brave men he had served with. Men, he said, who had made the "ultimate sacrifice." He spoke with respect for the Japanese—though he called them Japs—who would die rather than surrender. He spoke again of the brotherhood of veterans.

When I finally decided I should leave, Mr. Conradt asked me a favor. He wanted to know if he could keep the guns overnight. He knew Mr. Roberts would be equally thrilled to see the weapons. I thought about how this was the most energized I had ever seen Mr. Conradt. I was sure Dad wouldn't miss the guns.

"I'll make you a deal," I said.

"Name it."

"Let me hold on to that picture of Mrs. Conradt, just for a while."

"What on earth for?"

"I think I can do it now," I said. "I think I can ask out Jenny. If I can ever get a minute alone with her, that is."

"So what's the picture for?" he asked as he fished it out of his chest and handed it to me.

"Inspiration," I said. I slid the photo into my wallet. He just laughed.

My dad woke me up early the next morning. Real early. Still-dark early. At first I was too groggy to really understand anything he was saying. It was something about the guns. I hoped I wasn't in too much trouble.

"I'll get them back today," I said. "Mr. Conradt wanted to see them."

"Wake up, Jeff," Dad said. He shook me. "Something terrible has happened."

I never saw Mr. Conradt again. They wouldn't let me, though I would have liked to say goodbye.

The bullets, they said, were in a small metal lockbox in his war chest. Fifty-year-old bullets that still worked. No one came right out and said it, but I knew what people were thinking. Stupid kid. How could anyone be that dumb? The newspaper accounts left out my name, but everyone in school knew what had happened. I didn't talk about it, though. At all.

They rented two Greyhound buses when we made it to the state quarterfinals in basketball. On the way to the game, the team rode on one bus and the dance team and cheerleaders rode in the other. After the loss, they didn't care which we rode on the way back. I boarded the first bus available and made my way to the last row of seats. I closed my eyes and tried to disappear for twenty or thirty minutes. Then someone tapped me on the foot.

I opened my eyes. It was Jenny Robinson.

"Sorry about this. I think you're laying on top of my purse."

"Oh, uh . . . yeah. I'm sorry."

I sat up, and she grabbed the leather bag.

"You played great."

"Thanks."

She sat down. At first I felt awkward, but we started talking right away. She wanted recommendations on what to take next year. She was still a junior. She asked whether I was going to try to play basketball in college. I found out we were both *X-Files* fans. She was really nice. We were reminiscing about a cat dissection unit in biology—the one class we'd ever had together— when one of her friends called her up a few rows for some bit of gossip.

While she was gone, I took the photo of Mrs. Conradt out of my wallet. Such a beautiful woman. I didn't notice when Jenny returned and sat next to me.

"Cyd Charisse," she said.

"What?"

"What are you doing with a picture of Cyd Charisse?"

"Who's Cyd Charisse?" I asked.

"Movie star in the forties and fifties. A great dancer too. My gramma was a big fan of old movie musicals. Gene Kelly. Fred Astaire. She and I used to watch 'em all the time on AMC weekend matinees. Cyd Charisse costarred in a lot of those films. She was very pretty."

"Yeah," I said, looking down at the photo. "She was."

I wondered if, somewhere in a minimum-security prison in the Panhandle, Mr. Conradt was watching TV in his cell with a big, self-satisfied smirk on his face. I wondered, like I had so many times already, if he shot Mr. Roberts because of the Alzheimer's. A "mercy" killing, like he said. Or if he just saw himself, his own decline, in his war buddy and couldn't stand to look at it any longer. Mostly I wondered if, to him, I'd been anything more than a tool.

The bus pulled into the Lee High parking lot. The dance team and cheerleaders had already recovered from the defeat and were giggling and screaming as they gathered their things and exited. Jenny handed the photo back to me, and I felt her fingers graze against mine. I could've sworn she let them linger there.

But then again, I probably imagined it.

ROB THOMAS, the author of *Rats Saw God* and *Slave Day,* taught high-school journalism for five years; advised the staff of the University of Texas student magazine, *UTmost;* and worked for *Channel One* in Los Angeles, a television news show aimed at teenagers nationwide. He lives in Austin, Texas.

"In high school," he says, "I was a member of the Key Club. One of our ongoing service projects was writing birthday cards to the residents of a local retirement home. The director of the home asked us on several occasions to come and visit the patients, but the thought of meeting them in person made me uneasy. It wasn't that I was afraid of old people; I wasn't. What really bothered me was the presumptuousness of it. Would the residents feel imposed upon by a group of high school do-gooders? Would they be interested in anything we talked about? Finally, would they know deep down that we viewed these visits as some kind of charity work? 'The War Chest' was one of my darker musings about how this teen volunteer–elderly patient relationship might play out."

EAT YOUR ENEMY

by Nancy Springer

I t was June, and the kitchen of the Virginia farm-house had no air-conditioning, but Cassidy started shivering as she hadn't all through the drafty winter. Her father, laying the handguns on the table, glanced at her from under the brim of his Washington Red-skins hat.

"You scared?"

She shook her head. She didn't feel scared; she didn't feel any emotion at all. Just cold for no reason.

In general she hadn't felt much emotion since Mom died.

"They're not loaded," Dad said.

"I'm not scared."

"Okay. Well, this is an antique, a big old .45 re-volver like the cowboys used to carry. This is a .44 Magnum like Clint Eastwood waves around. Too much gun for you. This is a .38 revolver. That would be better." He pointed out the pistols with his steady callused forefinger; his hands were rough and grimy from sanding gunstocks, setting barrels, welding, all the things a gunsmith does. "This is a little bitty .22 like the rich ladies tote in their purses. This is a 9-millimeter semiautomatic—"

All by itself her throat made a hurt-puppy sound. She felt her father looking at her as she sat on the cold old-fashioned radiator, hugging herself and shaking.

Dad asked very quietly, "Which kind did the mugger use?"

Cassidy wasn't sure. It had been six months since Mom was killed and she came to live with Dad; the bad memories—night, shadows, the man in the D.C. alley, her mother's panicky scream—were fading. She had only a dim picture in her mind of the pistol she had glimpsed from the corner of her eye. But she knew which gun had made her squeak.

She unlatched her right hand from her left elbow and pointed at the 9-millimeter.

"That's right. The police can tell from the bullet." Dad paused, tall and awkward, shifting from one Dingo-booted foot to the other. Finally he said, "Which one do you want to learn on?"

"None of them."

"Cass, come on." Dad sat down in one of the ladder-backed kitchen chairs and looked straight into her face. This was as close as he got to arguing. She'd never known him to raise his voice, even when he and Mom were fighting, splitting up. "You can handle this.

Heck, in another year you'll be driving a car. That's a lot more dangerous."

"I never said guns were dangerous."

"Then what's stopping you? Cass, you're my daughter. I want you safe. Just like I wanted you to learn how to swim so you wouldn't drown. I want you to learn how to handle a gun."

Suddenly without meaning to she was shouting. "What for?" She lunged to her feet. "Somebody tries to rob me, I shoot him? I don't think so!"

"Depends on the situation." Dad leaned back in his chair and spoke softly. "But if you know how to handle a gun, maybe he doesn't bother you in the first place."

"Oh, *really?*" She let herself be sarcastic.

"Yes, I think so. If you know how to handle a gun, it shows."

"And just how does it show?"

"Same way it shows that you can handle a horse."

She rolled her eyes. Dad had the weirdest ideas. He read too much.

Dad said, "I seem to remember when you were little you used to be scared of horses."

"I'm not scared!" But this time, even though she wasn't shaking anymore, she knew she was lying. She could feel the fear crawling like a lizard in her belly.

"Well, if you're not scared, then choose your weapon." When Dad got that quiet growl in his voice, it was final.

For a moment Cassidy almost hated him. Choose her weapon? Fine. She'd show him. She jabbed her finger at the 9-millimeter semiautomatic.

"That one?" Dad's voice went falsetto. She'd surprised him good.

She just glared back at him.

But then he surprised her; he smiled. "You have good instincts," he said. "Eat your enemy."

"Huh?"

"Something my grandmother used to say." Maybe he would have explained, but there was a sound of gravel crunching, a pickup coming down the lane. Business. Dad headed out the kitchen door toward the gun shop, a small log building out back under a black walnut tree.

Cassidy headed outside also, but not toward the gun shop. She never went in there.

From the cowshed on top of the limestony hill, Cassidy could see Dublin Malarkey grazing far down the pasture bottom. When she cocked her tongue against her front teeth and whistled like she was hailing a D.C. taxi, the big red Thoroughbred flung up his head and cantered toward her.

Cassidy watched, feeling her heart lift like her horse lifting to jump outcroppings of rock and rifts of thistles just for the joy of it. She felt her pulse speed to match the rhythm of his long-legged strides as he thundered up to her and jolted to a stop. He arched his sleek neck and stretched his head toward her, ears pricked.

"Hey, Lark." She fed him his reward, a gumdrop. She hugged his warm silky shoulders and laid her head against his tawny mane. So lucky to have him. Most horses, you try to call them, they look at you like you have seventeen heads. But Malarkey ran to her when she whistled because he loved her.

She brushed him, finding a bloody scratch on one flank from a tree or something. She sprayed antiseptic on the scrape. Back in D.C., when Malarkey was a show horse, he stayed in a stall all the time and never got a mark on him. Never got to run free, either. Now that he was out in the pasture there were dangers—he could get struck by lightning; about once a year it happened to somebody's horse. But the light in his eyes made the risk worth while.

She slipped the bridle on. No saddle today. Bareback, she rode at a walk up the lane and across the road into the apple orchard, where fallen petals lay like snow on the ground. Between the rows of trees she jogged him. Riding made her breathe easier, made her shoulders lift and spread like wings, her chest widen.

On her horse she could talk about whatever was on her mind. "Lark, I am so mad."

Malarkey flicked his ears and snorted.

"Dad has no right forcing me to shoot a gun. I despise guns."

Malarkey bobbed his head, resisting the bit. Gently Cassidy squeezed the reins to correct him.

"Dad's crazy. What do I need to shoot a gun for?
I'm not going to be a cop." Or a hunter, although she
liked eating the venison Dad brought home. "Or anything like that. Dad's just being a pain."

Malarkey quickened his trot, wanting to run. Cassidy knew she couldn't let him take charge. She was
the rider, she was responsible, she had to decide when
it was safe to go faster. "Lark," she told him, "don't be
a boogerhead." She increased contact until Malarkey
jogged quietly down the tractor path on the far side of
the orchard, his ears swiveling to listen to her, his
mouth listening to her hands on the reins.

"Dad's full of bull," Cassidy muttered.

An hour later, going home, she let Malarkey gallop
up the pasture hill to the barn. Wind in her hair.
Power pounding between her knees, hers to control.
With her expert, balanced seat on the horse, she wasn't
afraid of falling; she felt like she was skimming above
Lark, flying. She watched carefully in case she needed
to guide her horse around a woodchuck hole, but as
she watched she laughed for joy.

Jumping off Malarkey, patting him, she saw her father sighting in a rifle down below, aiming at a target
set up against a thick barrier of straw bales. One good
thing about Dad and all his guns, he shot the wood-
chucks to keep them out of Malarkey's pasture.

Cassidy blew breath between her lips in an exasperated sigh. Her father. The nicest person in the world,
and crazy about guns, always had been, loved every-

thing about them, the yellow-varnished wood, the blue metal, the oily smell, the cold steely feel, the click, the kick, the roar in his ear, everything. And she, Cassidy—she was crazy about her father. Always had been. Loved his quiet smile, his strong careful hands, his shy gray eyes, his stories, his lean jeans and muddy boots, his fricasseed squirrel suppers and wild goose soup. Loved everything about him.

Till now.

Malarkey sighed even harder than she did, fluttering his lips and nostrils.

"He can't make me," Cassidy told her horse.

"No," she told her father that evening when he said it was time for her first lesson. "I won't do it." He would never hit her or even yell at her, so what could he do? Push the gun into her hand?

They had just finished supper—deer burgers. Her father tilted his chair back from the table and studied her, sober-eyed. "Then I guess you can't ride Malarkey," he said.

"What? That's not fair! What does Malarkey have to do with—"

"Horseback riding is dangerous," her father said. "Look what happened to Christopher Reeve."

"It is not! I mean, it is, but—life's dangerous. That's not what this is about."

"Then what is it about?"

She didn't know what to say. Was she standing up for herself? Or was she just scared? She stared at him.

He got up from the table. "Come on," he ordered, and she followed.

Broken pieces of light fell in through the barred windows. The gun shop smelled like sawdust and solvent and gunpowder, smells that stung her nose. Everywhere were benches and tools that were strange to her. Her father showed her where the keys were kept for the gun cases and where the ammunition lurked in its drawer. He showed her how to get down her gun and keep it always pointed in a safe direction. "Even when it's not loaded. Get in the habit. Whenever anybody gets shot by accident, it's by a gun they thought wasn't loaded." He checked the pistol to make extra sure it was clear, then passed it to her, and even though she knew it was safe, her hands shook. Her head buzzed. She couldn't think.

She said nothing, but her father seemed to know. He put the gun back and locked the case. Outside, he locked up, then showed her how to disarm the security system with the number pad. "So you can get in if you have to."

"I won't."

"Honey, I hope you never need to, and that's the truth."

The next evening he showed her how to load the magazine with cartridges and ram it into the handgrip of the pistol. He showed her how to thumb the slide release lever and feed a cartridge into the chamber. The slide snapped into place with an angry click. "Up yours," Cassidy muttered. As long as she stayed mad she didn't shake. Her father looked at her but didn't say anything.

That night, sleeping restlessly in the June heat, she dreamed of the November darkness, the cold city street, Mom in her fur coat, blond as a movie star and all dressed up, walking home from the symphony, Cassidy beside her wobbling a little in heels as they passed the shadowy mouth of the alley and then—the harsh voice too close behind them—

Wake up! It's not happening, it's done, it's over.

She couldn't wake up. She couldn't do anything. She was helpless, standing there in her stupid heels as her mother panicked, spun around, and probably saw the guy's face, and then there was the flash of fire and the black explosion and the man running away and Mom on the ground and someone screaming and screaming—

Cassidy woke up screaming as her father came running into her bedroom in his sweatpants. "Cass! What's wrong?"

She was gasping, couldn't seem to get enough air. She couldn't answer.

He sat on the bed with her and held her against his chest and smoothed her hair with one rough hand. He was almost as big and warm as Lark. Her breathing calmed down, but she still leaned against him.

"Bad dream?" he murmured.

She nodded, lay down, and closed her eyes. Did not want to talk about it. She felt him touch her hair again. He sat with her so long that she must have fallen asleep; she did not hear him leave.

The next evening he made her go into the gun shop herself and take her handgun—unloaded, but pointed safely toward the air—a magazine and a box of ammo out to the targets while he followed with the eye goggles and shooting muffs.

"Okay," he said. "You ready to learn to fire your weapon?"

"No."

"C'mon, Cass, the sooner you get this over with, the sooner you'll feel better."

He showed her how to hold the unloaded pistol in a two-handed grip and aim at the target. "Keep that left thumb out of the way of the hammer or you'll be hurting." Then he positioned the eye goggles and ear protection on her head. "Lay the pistol down and put one cartridge in the clip. Just one."

She tried to do it. Her hands seemed to have turned to jelly. It took minutes for her to get the cartridge into the magazine, the magazine into the gunstock, the cartridge into the firing chamber. Her father waited patiently.

"Okay, take aim." As she lifted the handgun, he stood close behind her. "I'm right here."

Her ear protectors made him sound far away. The mugger, slipping out of the alley right behind her, had sounded nearer, and—it wasn't just fear that made her tremble; it was awe, enormity. *I am not big enough for this.* The gun was loaded. She could kill somebody.

"Hold your breath."

She did, but the pistol still shook in her hands.

"Focus on the sight at the end of the barrel."

She couldn't focus on anything. Her eyes were stinging, blurring.

"Okay, remember to squeeze the trigger, not jerk it. Fire when you're ready."

She would never be ready. She fired anyway. *Crack,* like the world breaking. Things flew up in a flurry—bits of straw, shell casing—as the pistol jumped, biting her hand. She wobbled, but her father's hands on her shoulders steadied her.

"Good," he said. "You hit within a couple feet of the target."

She slammed the gun down on the ground. "Where's a shovel?"

"Why?"

"I want to dig a hole and throw this pistol in and bury it."

"Load again."

"No."

"Yes. You might want to try two cartridges this time."

By the end of the second week she was hitting the target—not the middle of the target, but somewhere on the target—most of the time.

Dad had made her learn how to fire a gun. But he couldn't make her like it.

Daytimes she was mostly on her own. She had a few chores, and sometimes if Dad had to run errands, she rode along with him, but other than that he worked in his shop and she rode Dublin Malarkey.

After a rainstorm a fallen tree blocked the woods trail. Lark shied; Cassidy made him face the obstacle and jump it.

It was a green, wet June; the grass was tall, the river deep. She rode him across; he lunged in and swam against the current as she hung on, urging him forward.

She galloped him up the fire lookout tower trail, hands tangled in his mane, as he swept red as flame up the mountain.

When she rode, it was like the power of the horse surged into her. Sometimes she laughed out loud.

Sometimes she held her breath.

On an ordinary, boring end-of-June day, Dad asked her if she wanted to come with him; he had to drive over to Front Royal, look at some fruitwood a guy had for sale. She shook her head; she wanted to go riding.

The Dodge truck roared up the lane amid dust, then disappeared down the road as Cassidy headed out to the pasture. From the top of the hill, she saw Malarkey grazing far down the rocky slope near the pond. Her beautiful slim-legged Thoroughbred, sleek and red as a deer.

She whistled.

Malarkey flung up his head and galloped toward her.

The woodchuck hole lay hidden in the lush grass cupped between two ridges of limestone.

Cassidy saw it happen. She was watching Malarkey lilt toward her like a red bird on the wing, flying over rocks just for joy, bucking, tossing his head as his mane caught the sun, lifting to leap again—and in one crashing instant it all went wrong. Lark thudded down with a cry, a wrenching scream. As Cassidy ran toward him, he lunged, struggled, staggered to his feet—but he stood shuddering on three legs. He put no weight on his left forefoot, and below the knee the leg swung like a snapped twig.

Cassidy did not remember running the rest of the way to him, but she was there, her hands trying to comfort his face, but he was trembling, already slick with sweat, all the pride gone out of his flinching neck, his eyes blank and milky with pain. She stared—where the leg dangled, so wrong, she could see blood, a white jag of bone piercing the skin, and she knew there was nothing anybody could do. When a horse breaks a leg that way, it has to be killed.

Malarkey tried to step toward her and gave a grunting cry.

"No," Cassidy whispered. "No, Lark, don't try to

move. . . ." She stumbled back from him, turned, ran toward the house to call the vet, get somebody to come and put Malarkey down, end the agony.

But it would take the vet half an hour to get there, maybe an hour.

Behind her, Lark screamed again.

Running up the yard, Cassidy changed direction and darted toward the gun shop. Tears stung her eyes, but she blinked them back. She pressed the security numbers rapidly, got it right the first time. Opened the door. Grabbed the keys out of their drawer. Unlocked the gun case, grabbed the 9-millimeter semi, snatched ammunition, and loaded the clip and rammed it in and worked the slide to snick a bullet into the chamber and made sure the safety was on as she ran back down to the pasture.

Lark's red coat had gone white with foamy sweat. He stood shuddering, his eyes sunken and bewildered. He stretched his lank neck toward her, appealing for help.

She gave him the only help she could.

"I love you," she whispered—and then she thumbed the safety off. From barely two feet away, so she couldn't miss, she took aim at the center of his forehead, where the coppery hair parted in a whorl. She held her breath. Steady, steady. She sighted down the gun barrel. She squeezed the trigger.

An explosion like the end of the world. The thud as Lark fell.

Then silence except for the ringing of her ears.

He lay still. Didn't thrash around. She'd done it right.

She sat on the ground beside him and cried.

Malarkey wasn't beautiful anymore; just a grotesque oversized lump with clumsy hooves, tail strewn at an awkward angle. Only his mane was still beautiful. Cassidy stroked the golden hair flowing down.

"Mom," she whimpered.

She cried until she thought she was finished, and then she sat. For maybe an hour, maybe two—she didn't notice. She didn't see her father's pickup come into the driveway, and she didn't hear him as he walked up to her, just saw his boots as he stood there figuring out what had happened. She didn't look up at him as he knelt beside her, but when she felt his arms around her, she sobbed into the rough cloth of his shirt.

"God," he whispered as he patted her hair. "Oh, God, Cass, I'm sorry."

"I'm—I'm okay." She sat up and wiped her nose on the shoulder of her T-shirt. When she looked up at him, she saw that she was more okay at this point than he was. His face was gray with shock.

"God," he said, picking up the handgun from the flattened grass. "Cass, I—I'm so sorry. You don't ever have to touch this again if you don't want to."

His hands, usually so steady, were fumbling with the pistol. She reached over, took it gently from him, and checked the safety; she couldn't remember pushing it on, but she had. Good. She held the pistol in her lap, pointed at the ground.

She felt her father studying her.

She said to the gun, "I wasn't helpless. Not like—not like it was with Mom."

He sat down on the damp grass beside her.

She said, "I don't ever want to be helpless again."

She heard him take a long breath and let it out. Then he said, very low, "I keep thinking if your mom had been carrying a gun—but the truth is, it wouldn't have made a bit of difference. There was pepper spray in her purse, and she never used it."

"She panicked," Cassidy said. "I won't panic." She knew that now.

"That's true. But you could still get hurt."

"But at least I'd have some control. It's like horseback riding." She was unable to explain any further what she felt as she held the handgun.

She still didn't like guns. But she understood how her father could love them. How he could see beauty in them.

She reached out and stroked Malarkey's neck, touching that sleek hide one last time, cold now over his stiffened muscles.

She stood up and walked back toward the house. Her father walked beside her.

"I'll call a backhoe. We'll bury Lark." His voice went ragged. "We won't send him off to some rendering plant."

"Okay."

He nodded toward the handgun Cassidy carried. "You want me to clean that for you? Put it away?"

"No. I'll take care of it."

Silence for a moment. They walked on. Then he said, his voice steady now and soft, "You're going to do all right, girl. You know how to eat your enemy."

They were passing under the black walnut tree. She stopped and looked at him. "What does that mean?"

"My grandmother—you know she was part Shoshone." He meant his mother's mother, then. "She said if a rattlesnake tried to bite you, kill him and roast the meat. Eat the good and the strength of him. Leave the poison behind."

Cassidy went into the gun shop, cleared her weapon, and put the magazine and ammo away and sprayed the blue steel with Rem-Oil and wiped it with a soft rag. She cried while she was working, for Lark, for her mother, because she had to. But she was leaving the poison behind. She was thinking far ahead to when she would be grown, thinking about finding strength in a rattlesnake world and being the woman she wanted to be.

NANCY SPRINGER is a lifelong fiction writer with numerous publishing credits in a variety of genres:

mythic fantasy, realistic fiction, children's literature, mystery, suspense, short story, and poetry. Her fantasy novel *Larque on the Wing* won the James Tiptree, Jr. Award and was nominated for a Nebula. Two of her young adult mystery novels, *Looking for Jamie Bridger* and *Toughing It,* have won Edgar Allan Poe Awards. A resident of Dallastown, Pennsylvania, Springer teaches creative writing and, in her spare time, is an enthusiastic horseback rider.

Nancy Springer recalls that her father and two older brothers were hunters, and she remembers being allowed to shoot a rifle at a target when she was about ten. Her brother Ben remains an avid hunter, coaches riflery at Boy Scout camps, and at one time ran a gunsmith shop. The farm in "Eat Your Enemy" is based on Ben's farm in northern Virginia, and the character of Cassidy's father resembles him in some ways.

UNTIL THE DAY HE DIED

by Harry Mazer

Mike was falling. He was in the air, suspended from his parachute. He was alone, dangling, hanging like a spider in a web of ropes. Below him, he saw two other parachutes. No planes. The bombers had all disappeared. Nothing remained in that empty sky but three parachutes and a great column of smoke where the bombs had been dropped.

The brown dish that was the earth grew larger and larger. He heard—or maybe he only felt it—something rushing at him, like a whir of wings, a hissing. He thought it was a bird, and he looked up. There was a hole in the parachute. Then another. Someone was shooting at him. He threw his arms and legs around. Why would they shoot at him? He was coming down. He was surrendering. He wasn't going to hurt anyone.

He wished he could see the ones with the guns. He wished he could see their faces, and they could see his. He wished he could look into their eyes, the way he

looked into his mother's eyes, and they would see that
he meant them no harm. His mother's photo was in
his wallet. He wished it were larger so he could hold it
up to the ones with the guns, so they could see that he
had a mother and he was just a boy.

When the war began, Mike had been sixteen. He was
in high school, and the minute he heard about it, he
was ready to go. He knew about war from the movies.
He went every week and sat there with his mouth
slightly ajar, which he had a tendency to do when he
was excited. On the screen, ships were sunk, and men
were in the water and in lifeboats, and they were starting off on raids and missions, and there were explo-
sions and bombs going off, and smoke and shooting,
and men crouched over, dashing from one cover to
another. It was great. If he could have climbed into the
screen, grabbed a gun, and become part of the action,
he would have done it. He hated it when the movie
was over and he had to go out in the street.

It was always a shock, walking home in the dark, the
streetlights coming on, everything quiet except for an
occasional passing car, the hum from the factories on
the west side, and the periodic rattle of railroad cars
banging together. Everything so common and ordinary. He envied the older guys in the neighborhood
who were leaving every day, then coming back in their
uniforms like princes and lords. Sometimes, at home
with his parents and brother, he'd be listening to the

radio, listening to the war news, and he could barely keep still. What if the war ended and he was still here, still waiting to be old enough. When Don Beck, who lived a few blocks away on Grant Boulevard, went to Canada and joined the Canadian Air Force and was sent to England and saw action and returned with an airman's wings sewn to his tunic next to the ribbons he'd won, Mike could hardly breathe in his presence. He followed Don around. What he felt went beyond envy. It was awe.

He wanted to get into the war. He wanted to have a gun in his hands. A gun of his own. His father wouldn't allow guns in the house. His father's father had returned shell-shocked after World War I, unable to ever work again. "A burden to himself and his family until the day he died," Mike's father said. "War is the devil's work, an abomination and a horror."

He wouldn't even let Mike have an air rifle. And when Mike said how much he wanted to sign up, his father said, "You don't know when you're well off, laddie. Be glad you're too young. I pray every day that this war will end before it's your turn."

"Next year," Mike said. "When I'm seventeen, I'm going to sign up."

"You will," his father said. "But first you'll have to kill me."

They lived off Carbon Street in back of another house, he and his kid brother and his parents. His father was a laborer working on gas lines for Niagara Mohawk. He was shorter than Mike by a head and

darker, a compact solid man. He was like a tree. Once
he came to a conclusion, that was it. Mike didn't look
anything like his father. Mike was tall, bony, a redhead
with the pale coloring that went with it. He looked
like his mother, though he preferred to think he really
looked like the actor Gary Cooper.

At night, Mike and his friends ran the streets playing Commando and other war games, crashing
through privet hedges and back alleys. He was a Spit-
fire pilot, with guns blazing as he closed in on one of
those German 109s. He crouched, with his fingers
poised, the "enemy" in his crosshairs. "Ta, ta, ta, ta,
ta . . ." Guns killed the enemy. He saw himself
dodging bullets. They could never touch him. "Ta, ta,
ta, ta, ta . . ."

His friend Frank Dee had a twenty-two rifle of his
own, and Frank's father kept several deer rifles in a
rack in the cellar. The shells he kept in a locked metal
box, upstairs. Frank and Mike would go down to the
cellar, and Frank would hand Mike a carbine from the
rack, first making sure it was clear.

Mike worked the lever, checked the breech, then
raised the gun and sighted it. He sniffed the wood and
the oiled barrel. He put the gun to his shoulder and
sighted along the barrel, his cheek against the stock.
Frank handed him another of his father's guns, a
World War I Springfield rifle. Mike hefted the gun and
ran his hand along the smooth stock. It was hard for
him to give the gun up, it felt so good holding it. He

and Frank talked about his buying a rifle and keeping it here in Frank's house.

They did a lot of target shooting behind the baseball stadium, where the trains ran on top of a high embankment. They set bottles up as targets and shot at them until they'd used up all the ammunition. Walking back, it was understood that Mike got to carry the gun. He held it in the crook of his arm or over his shoulder. He could feel people looking at him approvingly.

He and Frank had long discussions about what they'd do if the Germans came. It would be a surprise attack, maybe a night drop of paratroops. But no matter what the time, the minute they knew the Germans had arrived, they'd drop everything and run to Frank's house. They'd get his father's ammunition and guns and go to North High, get up on the top floor, maybe on the roof, where they'd be able to look down and pop the Germans off like flies.

That summer, just before Mike turned seventeen, he and Frank got jobs at American Bowling. There were plenty of jobs because so many men had gone into the army. American Bowling didn't make bowling balls anymore. Now they made gun stocks for M1 rifles. The rest of the gun was made at Smith Typewriter on West Washington Street, where Frank's father worked. When Mike and Frank went out to lunch, they'd sometimes walk over to talk to Frank's father.

When school started again that fall, all Mike could think about was turning seventeen and being old enough to enlist. He could hardly hear anything the teachers said. All he could hear was the *rat-tat-tat* of machine guns being tested on the roof of Brown Lipe Chapin on West Fayette Street. The day of his birthday, he had his birth certificate with him, and after school he went downtown to sign up. Everywhere, in the windows of houses, he noticed the blue and yellow banners showing that someone from that family was in the service.

He brought the papers home for his parents to sign. His father refused to even look at them. "I passed the physical, Pop." His father walked out of the house. Mike followed him. "I'm almost eighteen."

"No," his father said. "No, no, no. Never. Not until Uncle Sam makes me. I'm not giving him my son."

Mike held the papers out to his mother. "Mom, please." He begged his mother, pleaded. His mother could never say no to him.

She kept looking at him. She had a graceful way about her, and just a tinge of red remained in her hair. Mostly, you saw it around her eyes. "I can't, honey." Her eyes seemed to get redder and redder. "I could never forgive myself if anything happened to you."

What was going to happen to him? Why were they so scared? He wasn't going to get hurt. Didn't they know that? He took the papers and went to his room. His kid brother was lying on the bed, reading a Superman comic. Mike sat down at his desk and practiced his father's signature. But that was as far as it went. He couldn't go behind his parents' back.

When he was eighteen, he and Frank and some other boys all received their draft notices at the same time. They went down for their physicals together. When Frank was asked what service he wanted, he said Coast Guard and ended up in an engineer company in the infantry. Mike stood very straight and said, "I want to be a fighter pilot, sir." They put him in the Air Force and sent him to Miami Beach, Florida, for basic training, and then to San Antonio, Texas, for testing.

He was turned down for pilot training. He cried when he didn't see his name on the list. They made him a mechanic on airplane engines. He worked nights and slept half the day. It was just like working in a factory, third shift at American Bowling. He volunteered for gunnery school.

The training in Reno, Nevada, was swift and intense. They started on the shooting range with M1 rifles. Mike was good with targets. Even with a shotgun, riding on the back of a moving truck to simulate an airplane, he popped off the clay ducks as fast as they careened up from hidden locations. He learned how to assemble and disassemble a .50-caliber machine gun, the name of each part, how to load the gun and clear it when it jammed, and how to fire it in the air. But what he really loved was the ball turret. He was training to be the ball-turret gunner on a B-17 bomber.

The training started on the ground in a stationary
ball and then moved to a real one on a B-17 bomber.
The ball was like a transparent egg hanging underneath the plane. To enter it, you slid through a door in
the floor of the plane. In the ball, Mike had to sit in a
crouching position, with his knees up and his head
against the door, which he locked from the inside. He
was too big for the space, but he wanted it.

He was assigned to a B-17 bomber: a four-engine,
propeller-driven plane, big, slow, and noisy. There
were ten men on the crew. Two pilots to fly the plane,
a bombardier to drop the bombs, a navigator to get
them home safely, and six gunners who manned
mounted machine guns that poked out from every side
of the plane and gave the bomber its name, the Flying
Fortress.

Their pilot was twenty-one. He was a very good
bomber pilot. He had wanted to be a fighter pilot, just
as Mike had. The pilot wore his officer's cap crushed
and cocked over one eye. Mike wore his overseas cap
tipped the same way. The copilot was twenty-eight,
the old man of the crew. All he wanted was to get
home and see his wife and new baby.

Mike loved the ball. There was no other position
like it. The ball bulged beneath the plane, and when
Mike was in it, he could rotate it independently of the
plane's motion. He imagined that he was a fighter
pilot. When he fired at the towed targets, they were
enemy fighters and he was closing in on them. In the

ball he sometimes felt he was in the cockpit of a fighter
plane, a P-40 or a P-51 Mustang.

The crew trained together in Alexandria, Louisiana,
then went to Lincoln, Nebraska, to pick up a plane to
fly overseas. Until that moment, they didn't know if
they were going east to fight the Japanese or west to
fight the Germans. But there was no question when
they flew to Bangor, Maine, then Goose Bay, Labra-
dor, then Reykjavik, Iceland. They were going to fight
the Germans.

They were based near a tiny village in England
called Royston, some miles north of London.

They lived in long steel Quonset huts. Inside, there
was a stove, a table, and enough beds, one on top of
another, for two crews. Being tall, Mike had an upper
bunk. On a shelf alongside his bed, he kept his stash of
cigarettes and goodies. At night when the lights went
off, the mice raced up and down the shelf and gnawed
through his packets of Lorna Doones.

On mornings when they flew, the alert came before
dawn. Everything excited Mike. The electric light that
hung from the ceiling, and the office clerk singing out,
"Okay, you yo-yos, rise and shine!" Mike was always
the first one out of bed. He reached for his pants and
shoes and went through the darkness to the mess hall,
which reeked of eggs, toast, and coffee. He never ate
on mission mornings, just drank coffee and took an
orange for later.

In the operations room, he sat in back with the

other gunners, trying to guess what the target would be before the operations officer pulled the curtain aside. There, on a wall-to-wall map of Europe, was the thin red line that tracked their path over Europe and to the target in Germany. Berlin, the capital of Nazi Germany, was the first target. A long flight, seven hours or more over enemy territory, and a dangerous target at the end.

That first morning they went out into the gray chill. Trucks took them to the pads where the planes were waiting. There was a lot to do before the plane took off. Parachutes and harnesses to load on, and the bulletproof vests called flak suits. The guns had to be put in place, and ammunition and bombs had to be loaded. In the bomb bays, bombs hung like fat waiting pigs. They'd be fused by the bombardier gunner once they were in the air. When Mike had finished his check of his position, he went up on the wings to check the fuel levels. When the pilots were ready, Mike got out in front and turned the props, then stood by as they began to rotate. The last thing he did was bend over and run through the prop-wash to pull back the wooden wheel chocks.

Takeoff was scary. The four gunners in back went as far forward as they could and sat with their backs against the bomb-bay partition. The plane, loaded with bombs, ammunition, oxygen tanks, and men, lumbered down the runway. Mike had heard stories of planes that would run and run, maybe half lift into the air, and then crash. He didn't like to think about the bad stuff.

There were other dangers, as well. It was dark and foggy, and there were too many planes in the air. Everyone was on alert until they were in the clear. Mike stood looking out the side of the plane, ready to warn the pilot if another plane came too close. Slowly they climbed into the half-dark, early-morning sky. It was dawn, and they rose higher and higher, into the light above the clouds, like hawks circling up into a chimney of air.

On that first mission, Mike watched and was absorbed in everything. He was amazed as the bomb groups assembled. There was nothing in the sky but bombers. Each plane had an assigned position to fly. The bombers were staggered like steps on a staircase so that the guns of one plane could defend another. On signal, the armada, like a flight of giant birds, turned to the continent of Europe, climbing steadily on the long flight to Berlin. When they were over 10,000 feet, Mike checked his oxygen tank and hooked on his oxygen mask. He wore an electric suit, flight coveralls, and a flight jacket, and over that his parachute harness. The parachute he left by the door when he went down into the ball. There was no room for it below. If he had to bail out, he would have to come back into the plane, snap on the chute, and then jump.

Squeezed into the ball, he rotated it slowly. They were now almost at 30,000 feet. He kept checking his oxygen mask and gauges. He could feel the moisture collecting inside, and he wiped his chin to keep it dry. Through a haze, he saw the English Channel and, ahead, the irregular edge of the continent of Europe. He thought how lucky he was to be here. It was a long way from home and Carbon Street.

He saw Holland and the Zuider Zee. The engines droned on. The bombers trailed long, chalky vapor trails from their wing tips. Flak burst below them, little puffs of black cloud. Mike saw it, without realizing what it was. The drifting puffs of smoke reminded him of the dry puffballs he used to step on in the autumn fields. But it was flak, and he was delighted: They were being shot at; they were in combat. He was almost joyous when he called it out on the intercom. "Flak, low at five o'clock."

Fighter planes—their own—appeared and disappeared, the graceful P-38 Lightnings and the powerful P-51 Mustangs. There were no enemy fighters. As they came over Berlin, the flak got heavy. Everywhere, he could see it rising to their altitude, black smudgy smoke climbing toward them. Sometimes it was so close it shook the plane. The plane rose and fell, trying to throw off the flak. Bags of bright metal chaff streamed from the planes to confuse the enemy radar. The chaff spilled like snow petals from the bellies of other bombers. It was almost like a wedding or a celebration.

Berlin lay below them like a huge black iron waffle. Mike swung the turret. In the distance—it was down, maybe four o'clock—he saw a B-17 split in half and fall away in two pieces, the tail spiraling like a floating leaf. A dot and a second dot fell from the front half of the plane. Dots, no larger than periods on a sheet of paper. Men falling without parachutes. He felt something in his stomach he hadn't felt before. Something hard and choking. He wasn't afraid, but that feeling, that heavy lump inside, didn't go away. It was with him, from then on, every time they flew a combat mission.

Mission after mission Mike turned, rotated, "flew" the ball. He watched for enemy fighters that never came, studied the sky hour after hour and saw nothing. Nothing to shoot at. Nothing to do but watch and worry. It was flak that they feared on the bomb runs. Flak was the enemy. It lined that final corridor, the gauntlet they had to run straight toward the target.

They were lucky. Coming late into the war—that was luck. They'd avoided the German fighters that had swarmed around the bombers in the early days of the war. Instead, they had flak, ragged bits of metal that bit and tore and ripped planes and men apart. Mike carried a piece of flak that had come through the Plexiglas and dropped, hot and sizzling, into his lap. It became his good-luck charm, and he never flew without it.

In the ball, under the plane, Mike saw everything. He saw the antiaircraft shells bursting below, coming closer. He saw the bomb-bay doors open. He saw the bombs elbowing one another, as they spilled out of the plane. He felt the plane lighten and spring up. He saw the bomb-bay doors close. "Bomb-bay doors closed," he confirmed over the intercom. "Let's get the hell out of here."

In those long, droning, dreary, weary hours, he amused himself by singing above the engine's drone, letting his voice rise and rise, feeling the astounding power of himself. He might have been in a cathedral, his voice filling the high vaulted spaces.

More and more now, he thought about getting through, finishing his missions and going home. The flak was coming closer all the time. On their last mission, the front-end gunner had caught a piece of it, and he was still in the hospital. Their plane had been hit so many times that it was pockmarked with aluminum patches. Mike remembered what his father had said. "Just hope you're too young for this war and too old for the next." Well, he hadn't been, but his luck had held out. It only had to hold out a little bit longer. The war, everyone said, was coming to an end.

On their twenty-second mission, a German jet, a twin-engined ME-262, flashed through their formations. Mike screamed out its position, then fired and fired. He knew he fired, but afterward he couldn't remember actually doing it. The jet was there and then it was gone. "I hit it," he said. He couldn't stay off the intercom. "I'm sure I hit it. I know I did." But the more he said it, the more he doubted that he had hit anything. Nobody had seen the German plane trail smoke or show any damage. Who had even seen it besides him? It was like a dream. It was almost as if he'd created it so he could shoot it down. All he remembered was the swastika, black and crooked, on the tail. It seemed to him to stand two stories high.

There was a period where they didn't fly at all. For two weeks, they dug ditches and policed up around the huts. At night they played cards by the stove in the hut. Mike wrote letters to his parents and a girl he'd met in Louisiana. He wrote them both almost the same letter about an English bike he'd just bought and how he liked to ride it along the narrow, curving country roads. He told his mother that what he wanted when he came home was a big dark-chocolate cake and a quart of ice-cold milk.

On the night of April twenty-fourth they got word that they were going to fly the next day. Sometime during the night, Mike woke. He heard the *ping* of the stove and saw the glow inside trying to get out through the cracks. Mice ran unimpeded along the shelf near his head. He thought about the next day and wondered where they were going.

In the morning it was dark as they dressed. Mike wasn't hungry. He got to the briefing room early, sat in back, and waited for the briefing officer to pull back the curtain. Where could they go? The Russians were outside Berlin, the German capital, and the American and British armies were cutting deep into Germany. Hitler was caught. The door was slamming shut. As

for the big bombers, where could they attack without
the risk of hitting their own men?

But when the curtain was drawn, there was the red
line, running across France and the Alps and into
Czechoslovakia. Pilsen was the city they were bombing, their target the Skoda Munitions Works, a giant
arms and munitions center. Heavy flak was expected.
And one thing more. On this mission, all flight per-
sonnel would be issued sidearms and shoulder holsters
to be worn under their flight jackets. Too many reports
had been coming back of downed airmen attacked,
beaten, and hanged from telephone poles along the
highways.

On the way to the plane, Mike felt cold, and he
zipped up his jacket. The forty-five was a weight under
his arm. He was aware of it as he went through his
routine, felt it as he squatted on the wing and checked
the fuel. During takeoff, he sat with the other gunners
with his back against the bomb bays. He'd been
through this so many times now, but still he held his
breath as the heavy-loaded plane started down the runway. It was a relief when they were airborne. Every
step completed was a danger passed.

As they climbed—they were crossing the English
Channel—he hooked his oxygen mask to a portable
bottle and continued to watch out the window. He'd
be glad when this mission was over. Everywhere he
looked, he saw B-17s, hundreds of them all facing the
same way, moving like a school of fish through an
ocean of air. It was a perfect spring day, blue skies and

white clouds. It was hard not to feel good. There was some talk on the intercom, but as they neared the target, the talk ceased, and he went down into the ball. Ahead of them, in the distance, other bomb groups were approaching the target. Flak up ahead. He turned the turret. Flak stained the sky. The tail gunner's voice came over the intercom. "Flak at six o'clock."

On the final approach—the bomb run—the flak got more intense. Mike felt as if all the enemy antiaircraft guns were aimed at them. "Bomb-bay doors open," he called. He waited for the bombs to drop, but they never did. Maybe clouds obscured the target. They had to circle around and make a second run. Nothing like this had ever happened to them before. Mike wet his lips. He gripped his lucky piece of flak and prayed.

On the second run, their plane was hit. One moment they were steady, the plane level, engines droning, their ship riding neatly in its wing position. The next moment they were on fire. Mike felt as if they had run into another plane. He saw the wing on the port side crumple and fold almost against his turret. The plane wavered, then, like a man whose legs had been chopped off, it fell.

Mike swung the ball around and climbed up into the waist. He couldn't stay on his feet. He was thrown around. His oxygen hose flapped loose. He looked for a spare oxygen bottle and for his parachute. There was smoke and the smell of burning. The plane was tipping, dropping. He was pinned against the side. The waist gunner was crouched by the door, tugging at the emergency hinges. The radio operator's head lay in a little wet pool in the doorway of the radio compartment.

Mike crawled toward the door, fumbling with his parachute. The waist gunner was in the doorway, and then he was gone. Mike was having trouble focusing. No oxygen. He pushed himself to the door, closed his eyes and fell out.

Falling . . . He was falling. It was like nothing he'd ever felt before. It was almost like he was tumbling down a hill. Only it wasn't that. It was more like floating, like he was lying on a mattress. Only it wasn't that, either. His goggles hung by one strap and were hitting him in the face. There was pain in his ears. He was falling. He remembered he was supposed to count to ten before he pulled the chute. *One . . . two . . . ,* he counted.

He was falling. He didn't know how long or how far. They'd been five miles high when they were hit. He fell. Maybe he fell a mile, maybe two. He was above clouds, aware of them, aware that they were coming closer, and then he was in them, and they were all around him. He thought if anyone was watching from above, all he would see would be a black dot against a white background.

Mike didn't remember how he released the chute. What he was thinking was that he didn't know where the ground was, and he must have done something, because suddenly a dark tangle of cloth and rope flew into his face, and the parachute burst open. The force of it opening yanked him upright like a hand tearing open his chest, and he was gone, blacked out.

Pain woke him. He didn't know if he was alive or dead. He was in the sky, and he thought for a moment that he was on the way to heaven, but it hurt too much. There was pain in his head and pain in his crotch. A pale umbrella was opened above him. His legs dangled uselessly. The pain was from the harness straps digging into his crotch. He gripped the heavy shrouds over his head and pulled himself up to ease the pressure.

It was a beautiful, sunny day in April. He had come from smoke and noise, and now he was drifting in this blue, blue sky. No planes. Only two other parachutes far away. And someone was shooting at him. He kept looking around to see where the shots were coming from. It seemed so strange. They didn't even know him. He was just a man falling in a parachute. They didn't have to be afraid of him. He wasn't going to fight. Hadn't they heard that the war was almost over?

He remembered the gun in the holster under his arm. He freed it. He had trouble getting it out. It felt good having it free and letting it drop. Now they could see he meant them no harm. He was unarmed. He was done shooting.

The earth was reaching up, closing all around him. He could see fields along the side of a hill, and trees and cottages surrounded by gardens, and people outside running and looking up. He saw everything. He saw that he was coming down in a farmer's field, a big square field. Next to it was a cemetery surrounded by a low stone wall. On the other side of the cemetery was a road, and he saw a green car moving slowly along that road. He thought how beautiful it all was, and peaceful, all lying there before him like a sweet spring morning. He was floating down safely. He wanted to wave to the people coming to meet him. It was luck that had saved him and brought him to this place. It had to be luck, or God, or his mother's love, or his father's protective hand. All of it, perhaps. There was no other way to understand it.

AUTHOR'S NOTE

In the closing days of World War II, the Eighth Air Force flew its last heavy bombing mission in the European theater. It was April 25, 1945, thirteen days before the war in Europe ended.

The bombing target was the Skoda Munitions Works in Pilsen, Czechoslovakia. Six hundred planes set out on that mission. Two planes were shot down. The real Mike Brennen's plane was one of them.

Three men parachuted out successfully. Two survived: William D. O'Malley, Jr., and I. I had always believed that Mike went down with the plane, that when I bailed out I left him behind. Deserted him. He was my best friend, and his death has haunted me for all these years. It was only recently when I went back to Pilsen, Czechoslovakia, that I learned that Mike had also bailed out of the airplane and landed successfully.

Two members of the Luftwaffe, the German air force, captured me. They may have felt some sympathy for a member of even an enemy air force. My luck. Mike wasn't so lucky. Witnesses to his descent saw him land in a farmer's field next to a tiny Catholic cemetery. A Wehrmacht officer, a captain in the regular German army, stood there waiting. He killed Mike on the spot.

Mike and the rest of our crew, who had died in the crash, were buried in an unmarked grave inside the wall of that Czech cemetery. Lilacs now grow there profusely.

HARRY MAZER, the editor of this anthology, is an acclaimed author in his own right. His autobiographical novel about World War II, *The Last Mission*, was selected as an ALA Best Book for Young Adults and a *New York Times Book Review* Best Book of the Year. ("Until the Day He Died" tells part of *The Last Mission's* story from another point of view.)

Harry Mazer is also the author of *Snow Bound, Who Is Eddie Leonard?* (an ALA Best Book for Young Adults), *The Island Keeper, and Someone's Mother Is*

Missing. He and his wife, novelist Norma Fox Mazer, are the authors of *The Solid Gold Kid* (an ALA Best Book for Young Adults and an IRA-CBC Children's Choice), *Heartbeat* (an ALA Quick Pick and an IRA-CBC Children's Choice), and *Bright Days, Stupid Nights.*

The Mazers have four grown children and divide their time between Jamesville, New York, and New York City.

FRESH MEAT

by Ron Koertge

We shot deer, buffalo, and elk. We shot brown bears and grizzly bears. We shot alligators and crocodiles, elephants and rhinos. We shot sparrows and hummingbirds, knocking them out of the air with a bullet in the eye. If it swam, crawled, or flew, we shot it. And when everything in the whole wide world was dead, we shot each other.

Of course, we were only ten years old. And we didn't have real bullets. Or real guns. And the whole wide world was Bradleyville, Missouri. Or maybe just Eckart's pasture.

Part of it was sloping and smooth, all summer knee-deep in fescue and weeds that ran down to meet maybe an acre of walnut trees. The other part of the pasture looked like a giant tomahawk had come out of the clouds and opened up a huge wound in the ground. A wound that had scabbed over and tried to heal, but still oozed. Especially at night.

So Eckart's was a perfect place to play. I could almost get lost, I could hide from my friends for just about as long as I wanted, and I could get really dirty.

J.J., Pam, and I went to the pasture almost every day. Even when school started and it got colder and we had chores to do or homework, we usually found ways to spend a little time there. We all carried guns. Ones that shot caps or just clicked. Or we picked up a stick as long as a Winchester 76. Or made a revolver from scrap lumber. Or five fingers turned into a six-gun: The bottom three were the handle and trigger; the index finger was a barrel; the thumb became the hammer, always cocked and ready to fire.

I was the only one who had a real gun: a Savage single-shot .22. I got it for my birthday, but when I unwrapped it, the bolt was nowhere to be found. Not in another package, not lost in the brown wrapping paper with the mallards printed on it. Without a bolt, the rifle would never fire. It was like a car without an engine. A man without a heart.

"You can have the rest," my father said, "when I see how you handle this part."

He was serious, too. I had to carry the useless rifle around the house. It lay in the crook of my arm with the muzzle pointing at the floor. If I lifted it by mistake and pointed it at anything or anybody, it would be another month before I got the rest of the rifle.

When I wasn't carrying it, I could prop it up, but if it fell over, another thirty days would go by. Outdoors,

crossing a fence or resting, if a loaded gun slipped and
went off, somebody could get shot.

Everything about a gun was dangerous. Guns did
one thing: They killed. Owning and using firearms
was a huge responsibility. Everybody in Bradleyville
knew Mr. Clark, who'd been shot, accidentally, by his
own nephew on his first hunting trip.

My birthday was in September, and by October I was
allowed to show my friends the new Savage. They were
knocked out by it. The gun had a smooth and beautiful walnut stock. It was heavy and real. It even smelled
good, like oil and adulthood.

The first thing J.J. did was grab my rifle and point it
at a robin perched on a telephone wire. Then a squirrel
darted across the lawn. Pam was in between him and
it, so he swept past her, holding off until he had a clear
shot.

"Ka-pow!" He raised the barrel and blew away some
imaginary smoke.

Later my father and I were standing in the kitchen.
He said, "That boy is never to handle that weapon
again."

"Yes, sir."

"Not under any circumstances."

"Okay."

"You know why, don't you?"

"Yes, sir." And I did. J.J. was careless.

When Dad left the room, my mother said, "You don't look natural with that."

I shifted the rifle to my other arm, careful to keep the muzzle down. "I'm just not used to it yet."

"You could hurt somebody."

"Not unless I poked him in the eye with the barrel." I pointed to the empty chamber. "I don't even have a whole gun yet."

"After you do, you could."

"I'm not going to hurt anybody."

"In eight years, they'll draft you. Then *you'll* be the one somebody's hunting."

"The war's over," said my father from the other room. "Germany lost."

Mom grumbled, "The war's never over."

A couple of weeks after J.J. had waved my rifle around like a total jerk, I was down in the pasture by myself. I was just poking around, pretending I'd had a long day of hunting. I'd brought down a deer with a shot so perfect he dropped in his tracks and didn't suffer an instant.

I had bacon and some other stuff in my knapsack. I was going to cook and watch the sun go down. I'd just forked the bacon out of the little skillet and onto my plate when Pam turned up.

Pam was just one of the guys. She had really short hair, wore jeans and T-shirts. She cussed to show that she was tough. She wore her big brother's Roy Rogers pistols low on her hips, and she drew cross-handed. She was fast, too. With either hand.

She squatted down by the fire and held out both grimy palms to warm them up.

"Whacha eatin'?" she asked.

"Deer. But it tastes like bacon. Want some?"

"Nah." But she did. She was always hungry.

I held out the aluminum plate. "I can't finish it, anyway."

Pam hardly bothered to chew. "Man, this is good. What's in here?"

"Green peppers and onions."

"Your mom's a good cook."

"Yeah." That wasn't a lie; my mom was a good cook. She just hadn't cooked this.

Pam wiped her mouth with the back of one hand. "Wanna play Africa?"

"What's Africa?"

"It's a game I made up."

"Okay, I guess."

"Here's how it goes: My husband, Lord Oxford Bluebottom, just got killed by a lion."

I grinned.

"And tomorrow at dawn I'm going into the tall grass to find that lion. You're my husband's loyal butler, okay? And gun bearer. You know everything in the world about guns. Okay?"

"I guess."

Pam sat up straighter. She held out one hand. "Tea, please, Cuthbert."

"Cuthbert?"

"Shut up. That's you. Now, are you going to make tea or not?"

I took the little pan of water I'd been heating so I could wash up, and poured some in a collapsible cup.

She ordered me: "You say, 'Here you are, my lady. It's a pleasure to serve you and to do anything you desire any time of the day or night now that Lord Bluebottom is gone.' And kneel down. On one knee. And don't look at me until I tell you to and then you say kind of out of the corner of your mouth, 'Their eyes met!' Okay?"

I got to my feet. I felt weird. "This is stupid, Pam. I don't want to do this."

"No, it's okay. It'll get better. If you want, you can shoot the lion later on so he won't maul me to death. But we have to do this first. It's the rules."

"Whose rules?"

She jumped up. Her fists were hard as snowballs. "It's a game," she yelled. "All games have rules. You just think you're better than anybody else now 'cause you've got a rifle." She spit toward the fire. "What a joke. You can't even shoot it. All you can do is carry it around. And what good is it if you can't shoot anything."

I watched her run away. It was getting dark, but I could follow her dirty T-shirt as she zigzagged up the sloping pasture and disappeared.

*   *   *

Every Thanksgiving my aunts and uncles came to our house. Mom and I started a couple of days ahead of time, cutting onions and celery for the stock and making pans of corn bread for stuffing. Dad and I went to the market for pumpkin and marshmallows and cranberries and whatever else was on the long list that hung from our refrigerator door.

On Thanksgiving Day, Mom shook me awake at four o'clock in the morning. I pulled on some jeans and a sweatshirt, brushed my teeth, and stepped into the kitchen, which was already warm, already smelling good.

"Do you want coffee, honey?"

I shook my head, got down the eighteen-pound turkey out of the refrigerator, set her down in the clean sink, and let the water run.

Buying something from the market was sure easier than shooting it yourself. No buckshot to take out, no feathers to pluck. But I was careful, anyway. I felt the big cold breast for pieces of quill and reached inside, laying the liver and gizzard on the edge of the cutting board.

"How's the turkey?" Mom asked.

"Looks good."

I turned the carcass over one more time. I was careful with it. Polite, you might say. I listened during grace, all that "We thank You for this food" business. But I thanked the turkey by not slamming it around as if it'd never been anything but dead.

By the time I was done, the steamed-up kitchen

window was pink. Mom stopped crumbling up corn bread, and side by side we watched the day officially begin.

Then I took the big butcher knife and started to chop onions and celery. Outside, a pickup truck rattled by. Mom leaned, wiped steam off the window, and peered out.

I knew who it was by the bad shocks and ratchety engine: people named Wilson from down the street. Way down the street.

"He's going after rabbits, I'll bet."

Mom dumped out a pan of corn bread so hard, it shattered. "I hate guns."

"Mom, Mr. Wilson probably can't afford a turkey."

"I wasn't thinking about Mr. Wilson."

I leaned until my shoulder was touching hers. "When Dad let me sit on his lap and steer, you said I'd run into something." I held up the knife. "You always said I'd cut myself with this, and when I got that bow-and-arrow set you told me I'd hurt somebody, but none of those things ever happened."

I hung one arm around her neck and kissed her on the cheek. "You worry too much."

She put down the square tin pan and sighed.

I pulled at her apron, pretending I was going to untie the bow in the back. "Do you want me to make a green salad?"

"There's no lettuce. You'll have to go to the store."

"See, if I had a whole gun and some shells, I could go out and shoot some romaine."

Instead of laughing, she let her hands dangle in the sink. "I liked cooking with you."

"Why do we have to stop?"

"You'll stop." She looked at the corner. "If not right now, pretty soon."

None of my aunts and uncles—Karl and Edna, Doro and Lawrence, Willie and Eva—had any children. In the kitchen that afternoon, the women made over me—they liked my shirt or my smile or how tall I was getting. They praised my grades in school.

Usually, if I waited long enough, they forgot I was there and talked in half whispers about their bodies: how they felt, what hurt, what stopped hurting. "Do you, too?" they whispered. "I don't think he knows how much . . ." "The doctor said . . ."

But this year they noticed. Their murmurs turned to whispers. "Go in the living room, honey," Aunt Doro said. "Just for a little while, okay?"

"Why?"

They turned their backs on me. "Just go on. See what's on TV."

The men were watching football, not because they liked sports or followed any particular team. They watched for the same reason we were about to eat turkey: That was what you did on Thanksgiving.

Over the announcers and the spectacular end runs, they talked about cars, business, and money. And they talked about hunting. They wanted to shoot pheasant

in North Dakota, doves in Mississippi, deer in Colorado.

"I've got a new gun," I said. "Can I show them,
Dad?"

"All right."

A minute later, I walked back through the living
room. The bolt lay on the coffee table. I looked at my
father. He looked back.

Willie held the rifle up, sighted through the empty
barrel, nodded his approval. Then he slipped the bolt
in and locked it down.

It worked! The hair on my arms stood up.

Uncle Karl hefted it, let it balance in one hand.
"How's it shoot?" he asked. "Is it true?"

"I don't know."

"Well, let's find out then."

"After dinner," said my father.

I couldn't believe it. "You've got shells for it?"

"I could probably come up with a few."

Dinner was, well, dinner. Everybody said the same
things they said last year about the same food. Everybody ate a lot. Everybody but me. I took a little of
everything, but I chewed slowly and turned down seconds. The rest of them could get sleepy. Not me. I
wanted to be sharp when I handled the gun. Alert. At
my best.

But it seemed like they forgot. The women put on
their aprons and cleaned up. The men sat stunned as

yet another bowl game raged on Channel 5. I pretended to read a magazine, then a schoolbook. Uncle Willie snored.

Then my mother and her sisters all came into the living room. They stood in a line.

"We've been in the house all day," Doro complained. "Let's go for a ride or something."

"We're going down to Eckart's to shoot," Dad said nonchalantly. "You could come along. Plenty of fresh air down there."

"Couldn't we do something else?"

"Not right now."

The sisters looked at each other. "Oh, all right."

Uncle Karl had a Buick big enough for all of us. He dug in his gabardine slacks. "You know how to start a car, don't you, son?"

"Yes, sir. Dad showed me."

"Well, go out and warm up the Roadmaster for the ladies, okay? Just push the temperature gauge all the way over. Don't touch anything else. Leave it in Park."

"All right."

The steering wheel was huge. The dashboard like a cockpit. Even the keys were heavy, and when the engine turned over, I stopped breathing for a second. I just sat there imagining what it would be like to be able to drive, to go anyplace I wanted anytime I wanted.

With heat pouring out of the vents, I ran back inside, got my heavy jacket and gloves, picked up the rifle, clicked the safety on, walked out to the kitchen.

My father wore brown boots and a green hunter's coat with deep pockets stained red. "Everything okay?" he asked.

"Uh-huh."

"Let me see your rifle." I handed it over, and he checked the safety. "Good."

We drove the mile or so to Mr. Eckart's. I sat in the back between my mother and Doro, lost in their fur coats, half dizzy with the Shalimar perfume they all got for every birthday.

Karl parked the Buick in the big drive that led to the barn. Dad got out.

"C'mon, son," he said to me.

We walked to the back door together. When Mr. Eckart came out, Dad took off his cap and they shook hands. They talked about the dinner they'd just eaten, the weather, and the look of the sky.

I liked standing there with my father. If you wanted to hunt on someone's land, this is what you did: You drove up to the house and asked his permission. Even if, like us, there wasn't going to be any hunting.

"Sure," Mr. Eckart said. "Anytime."

"We've got some women with us," my father said like that meant something.

"Sure," said Mr. Eckart like he understood what that meant.

Because Aunt Doro insisted, Karl drove the car another hundred yards or so; then we all got out.

My uncles, my father, and I made a ragged line a

long way in front of my mother and her sisters. They followed, picking their way along carefully.

Both my uncles had shotguns. They always carried them, broken down, in the trunks of their cars along with boots and jackets.

We walked without saying anything. I'd hunted before I had a gun, just taking my place in the line, trying to scare things out of hiding. But if something jumped out right in front of me that day, I didn't know what I'd do.

Luckily, the rabbit we flushed out of an old shock of corn ran left to right: first past my father, then me, then Uncle Willie. Karl, last in line, brought his twelve-gauge to his shoulder and pulled the trigger in one fluid move, hitting the ground yards in front of the rabbit, but close enough to make him turn and dart the other way.

Behind me, the women put their gloved hands to their ears.

"Good shot, Karl!"

It was, too. He had missed on purpose. We didn't need the meat.

Down where the pasture started to get narrow and steep, Mr. Eckart had a kind of junk pile. There was part of a rusty harrow, a huge tractor tire from an old John Deere, a bedspring, a couple of oil drums, and dozens of cans and bottles.

"If you were going to shoot," my father asked me, "where would you put the targets?"

I looked around before I said anything. "Up against that slope."

He nodded. "Set up some of those cans."

When I came back, Dad handed me a box of .22-caliber bullets. The second thing I liked was how heavy the box was. The first thing was their color—dull brass and lead. They seemed different. Not of this world. Like kryptonite, maybe.

"Let your uncles shoot first."

"Yes, sir."

They tried out my rifle. They plinked cans off the ground, aimed for the peach on the label and hit it, aimed at the *O* on the Oxydol package and came close.

My mother called to me. "Honey, are you cold?"

I shook my head.

Uncle Willie handed me the rifle. "This is a nice .22, but off just a hair, so cheat a little to the left."

Karl sauntered over and lined up some cans for me. I slipped a shell into the chamber, shoved the bolt home, clicked the safety off, and waited.

Everybody watched me lift the rifle, snug it into my shoulder, aim, and squeeze. The green S&W can rocked, then fell off the branch it'd been balanced on.

"Nice shot," said Willie. Karl and my father both nodded.

I hit the next six in a row, and the six after that except for one, and that was my fault.

"Is that all you're going to do?" said my mother

suddenly. "Shoot at things standing still? Anybody can do that." She bent down, careful to not let the hem of her good coat reach the dirt, and picked up a beer bottle. She tossed it my way. "Hit that on the fly."

My dad cautioned her. "Now, Mother."

"If he's so good at this," she snapped, "if you're all such mighty hunters, why can't you hit something that isn't helpless."

My uncles looked at each other, then at the ground. They were embarrassed for my father.

I pointed toward the grove of walnut trees. "If you throw it *that* way and I miss," I said, "it won't matter."

"*If* you miss," said Aunt Edna. "That's a laugh."

I looked at my father. "Why is everybody mad all of a sudden?" I asked.

He turned the beer bottle over in his hand. "I'll toss it yonder, but pretty near straight up. Right before it starts down, that's your best chance."

I slipped in another shell. Everyone stepped back. Dad bent his knees a little, then lobbed the bottle up and out.

In the years since, I've tried this same shot more times than I like to admit, and the rifle just feels like a fireplug under my arm and the bottle spins crazily and catches the sun and blinds me.

But that day the gun was as much a part of me as my arm. The bottle flew and paused; it posed in the air. I blew it to smithereens.

Nobody said anything for a second. Then my uncles turned and shook hands. They laughed and slapped each other on the back.

"You couldn't do that again in a million years," cried my mother, wiping at her eyes.

"Try," said my aunt digging in her purse. "I'll bet a dollar you can't do that twice."

I looked at her little boots, the tops ringed with fur that she'd bought from a store.

"Do what I tell you now." Doro shook the money at me.

"No, thank you," I said. And I went over and stood with the men.

RON KOERTGE was born in Olney, Illinois, and now lives in Southern California. A teacher at Pasadena City College, he is the author of seven novels for young adults, including *The Harmony Arms; Tiger, Tiger, Burning Bright* (an ALA Notable Book and Best Book for Young Adults); *Confess-O-Rama;* and *The Arizona Kid,* which was selected by the American Library Association as "one of the ten funniest books of the year." He is also a published poet; his most recent poetry collection is *Making Love to Roget's Wife.*

Of "Fresh Meat," he says, "I was brought up around guns. The rituals of gun ownership—the period of waiting, the gun itself, the apprenticeship, the ceremonies of hunting on posted land—were all attractive to me. I liked the idea of being a good shot, but I wasn't so keen about being shot at, thus the title of the story."

CHALKMAN

by Rita Williams-Garcia

"Stay dead, Nkese."

How could she? Through squinty lids Nkese saw and felt Eamon hovering, breathing heavily as he scratched around her with that big old piece of chalk. She wanted to fall with her legs curled back in letter *J*s, but Rayquan took her by surprise, and she fell as usual in a heap holding her fake baby-belly.

"Nkese! You got to stay dead while I chalk you!"

She snuck in a final cheater's breath to sustain her while Eamon traced her outline. Eamon loved that chalk and could take forever, especially drawing Nkese. This only brought on a mad giggling impulse within her that followed the trail of Eamon's chalk, starting just outside her ear, up to the top braid of her "three-sies," down her forehead to the sloop! of her spunky nose, down her chin and neck until finally Nkese erupted.

"Dizzy girl! Can't stay dead for nothin'!"

Before he knew what he had done, Eamon threw down his chalk. Fat and round as it was, it neither broke nor chipped on the asphalt. Magic chalk.

With her eye on the chunky white stick, magic object of the game, Nkese sprang to life and snatched it, sealing it into the pocket within her knees drawn to her scrawny chest.

My chalk! Eamon thought, and that was all he thought when he stuck his hand into her cootie-laden girl parts to get it back. Nkese, bulldog-strong, kept herself locked around the chalk.

Eamon felt himself suffocating from the syrupy August air, the warm ring of laughter, squeals, and hoots of excited kids anticipating a fight. He also felt but ignored a flurry of rain punches from Njiri, Nkese's little brother, who wanted the third-grade bully off of his big sister.

Neither Eamon nor Nkese gave an inch. He forced her arm out in the open, but her fist remained tightly clinched. Eamon grunted and pulled, humiliated by the effort it took to subdue an eight-year-old girl whose chuckling now escalated to out-and-out laughter. He might as well have been tickling her. Dizzy girl! In a fit of panic he dug his runty nails deep into her skin, until her one eye teared and she screamed, letting the chalk roll out of her hands.

"I'm the Chalkman," Eamon told Nkese and everyone else who gathered around. "And you," he said, pointing down at her, " 'posed to be Miss Myra." With that, he took his chalk and broke up the game.

Shouts of "Demon Eamon, screaming like a baby" and "game killer" and "chalk stealer" and "can't beat a girl with a squirrel" (made up on the spot by Njiri) stuck to his back as he marched out of the playground, across the street, and up the steps of his house. Once inside the house with his chalk, Eamon didn't care.

He couldn't hear his friends, and they soon forgot him, having found some new game. Not a one of them looked up to catch him standing in his attic window tapping his head against the pane. Not one ran across the street to yell up at him.

As much as he wanted to rejoin his friends in the park, he couldn't bring himself to leave the attic window. He just stood there stiff-kneed, watching his friends as they hung upside down on the monkey bars until it rained and no one could play anything. The big kids who never let P.S. One-Thirty-Sixers near their sacred handball mural were forced to stop spray-painting. The girlfriend and boyfriend who were snapped together like Legos on the only good seesaw in the park separated and fled. The basketball court, also under big kids' rule, was empty, which made Eamon gloat as if he himself caused the rain and chased everyone out of the park. He hated the big kids. Especially the ones who saw you shooting hoops but usurped your court as if you weren't there. Not that his, Jimmy's, or Njiri's shots ever swished through the netted rim.

*   *   *

For the rest of that day Eamon sang victory songs to himself, happy that no one could play, but by the next day he was ready to run out onto Liberty Park with his friends. Again, he stood at the attic window pressing his head against the pane. The playground was still dead. Rain followed by damp after-rain days was the natural killer of outdoor kid fun. This is what Eamon, Nkese, Njiri, Jimmy, and Cherise knew as they stood at their respective windows staring out at the park, chanting with kid longing, "We want to play, we want to play." For all they knew, the whole world was damp and overcast. The good stuff, the slides, seesaw, and monkey bars were still wet.

They certainly couldn't play chalkman. Not even the fattest, most magical piece of chalk known to man-kind could write on dank city ground. The only thing rain was good for was washing away dozens of chalked figures to clear the ground for new games.

The Miss Myra-Toya-Scooter game was their favor-ite chalkman game because it required many players. There was a Darnell-Hines-Rest-in-Peace game not too long ago, but it wasn't as much fun, so they went back to the Miss Myra game.

At first they agreed to take turns being the Chalkman, Rayquan, Miss Myra, Scooter, Toya, and all the other parts, but Eamon would not relinquish his chalk since he found it and devised the rules of the game.

Only Eamon saw the man in the coroner's jacket drop the chalk inside the tire swing and only Eamon

rescued it. Then he drew his first outline and chased
Njiri and Toya around with freakish white hands.
Medicine men in New Zealand drew tribal markings
on warriors, though he doubted seriously if Nkese
would let him actually draw on her. One thing was for
sure. He'd never let Nkese hold his chalk any more
than Jimmy would let anyone hold his bike and Super-
Soaker to play Rayquan. Nkese always played Miss
Myra. And even though he didn't have a tricycle, Njiri
played Scooter by scrunching down and pretending to
pedal. Playing Toya didn't entail much, but Cherise
loved playing Toya because Toya had been her friend.
Everyone else claimed the remaining parts and the
game simply grew! It was bigger than *this-a-way Valerie, that-a-way Valerie*. Bigger than *slap, slap, clap, clap,
pat your baby on the back*. Yes. Even bigger than
dodgeball and freeze tag combined.

Then, just like in "The Itsy Bitsy Spider," out came
the sun, and Liberty Park was once again enraged with
the screams of excited children playing where little
children *could* play. All was forgotten the moment
Eamon saw Nkese, Jimmy, Njiri, and Cherise, the
main players, out on the monkey bars. He ran outside,
chest open, Demon Eamon with his chalk in his
pocket.

Teen mothers with strollers sat by the basketball
courts cheering on giants in high-tops leaping to the
suuuun! The big kids who called themselves artists

went back to their mural, repainting names within fluffy white clouds, the words REST IN PEACE, and ashened rose petals.

After rounds of sliding, seesawing, and chicken war, Eamon lead the shout for "Chalkman! Chalkman!" Then all joined in until enough players gathered around.

Fifth- and sixth-grade girls who usually clapped out the chalkman rhymes removed broken bottle glass from their game space. Nkese pushed a rubber ball up under her shirt. Njiri was on his pretend trykie. Cherise decided Toya should be playing make-believe jacks this time. She missed playing jacks with Toya. Jimmy was on his bike, ready to become Rayquan. Everyone else called out their parts.

"Game!"

The park was alive with hand-clapping, jumping, and hollering. The players had two minutes head start, though sometimes Rayquan cheated, surprising them. Rayquan was the only player allowed to cheat. Eamon said that was the way it was *supposed* to go. But if you made eye contact with Rayquan while you were "alive," you were out, so you had to keep jumping, hopscotching, freeze tagging, or whatever, until he came . . .

One-handed Rayquan ridin' on his bike
Whips out his Uzi, bullets start flyin'
batatatatatata-tow! batatatatatata-tow!
Down goes Miss Myra and her big old

belly
Down goes Toya and Scooter on his trykie
Rayquan still gunnin'
Everybody runnin'
rainy day
bullets spray
Rayquan rides away!
Well . . .
Callin' Mr. Operator, nine-one-one
Callin' Mr. Operator, nine-one-one

The EMS came, but they couldn't do
nothin'
The preacher man prayed but
they still dead
The camera man came but no one saw
nothin'
The police hit the scene and tried to
crack some heads
Along comes the Chalkman in the dead
body wagon
Took out his chalk and start to tag them
FREEZE!

This part took the longest. Eamon's part. First he did "Toya" because she was so little, and then "Scooter." He saved "Miss Myra" for last, although technically he should have done her first. This time "Miss Myra" contained her giggling impulse, though she wanted to fidget to throw off his neat white lines.

Zipped 'em up in body bags and
took them away!

Once their outlines had been chalked, the dead jumped up, formed a chain and followed the Chalkman in winding snakes all over the playground. Or they became free ghosts, sprang to life, and tagged everyone else dead. It depended on how long Eamon felt like playing, since he held the chalk, or if they could find a home base the big kids hadn't claimed.

Sometimes when they played chalkman, and died Miss Myra deaths, or Darnell Hines deaths, or Gimme-Your-Leather-Jacket deaths, they could see chalk bodies and chalk bodies and chalk bodies all over Liberty Park. By then, they'd be praying for some rain so they could start up new games.

RITA WILLIAMS-GARCIA is the author of the young adult novels *Blue Tights, Fast Talk on a Slow Track,* and *Like Sisters on the Homefront.* Her books have received numerous honors, including a PEN/Norma Klein Citation for Children's Literature, ALA Best Books for Young Adults and ALA Quick Picks listings, a *Parents' Choice* Honor for Storytelling, and a Coretta Scott King Honor Award. She works full-time as a manager of software reproduction at a marketing services company and lives in Queens, New York, with her husband and two daughters.

"A few years ago," Rita Williams-Garcia says, "I was visiting friends over the holidays when we heard the sounds of nearby gunfire. Even though the gunshots were perhaps blocks away, I pulled my youngest daughter close to me and ducked down. My friend's son, who was about nine, said, 'Capping. You hear that all night,' and continued playing with his race car.

"When I began to think of this story, I decided that instead of writing about the shooter or shooting victim, I would write about the kids who were touched—and untouched—by everyday violence."

KIDS AND GUNS:
THE STATISTICS

Sixteen children are killed with guns each day in the United States.

Every six hours, an American between ten and nineteen years old commits suicide with a gun.

More people between the ages of fifteen and twenty-four are killed with guns than by all natural causes combined.

Guns are the number one killer of African American men ages fifteen to thirty-four.

Gunshot wounds are the number two killer of all Americans ages ten to thirty-four.

A recent survey found that more than 1.2 million elementary-school-age latchkey children have household access to a gun.

A recent survey found that eighteen percent of suburban high-school students owned a handgun.

Another survey found that thirty-five percent of high-school students from high-crime areas carried guns regularly.

The gun you own for self-protection is forty-three times more likely to kill an innocent acquaintance than to be used for self-defense.

In one recent year, there were 13 handgun homicides in Australia, 33 in Great Britain, 36 in Sweden, 60 in Japan, 97 in Switzerland, 128 in Canada, and 13,495 in the United States.

(All statistics provided by the Center to Prevent Handgun Violence, Washington, DC, 1996)

IF YOU WANT TO
KNOW MORE

The following organizations are deeply involved in the issue of handguns as they affect the lives of young people:

Children's Defense Fund
25 E Street NW
Washington, DC 20001
(202) 628-8787

The Educational Fund to End Handgun Violence
110 Maryland Avenue NE
Box 72
Washington, DC 20002
(202) 544-7214

Center to Prevent Handgun Violence
1225 Eye Street NW
Suite 1100
Washington, DC 20005
(202) 289-7319